Youth:
Keeping the Balance

THE **mananam** SERIES

Youth:
Keeping the Balance

CHINMAYA PUBLICATIONS
CHINMAYA MISSION WEST PUBLICATIONS DIVISION

Chinmaya Publications
560 Bridgetown Pike, Feasterville Trevose, PA 19053-7240, USA
(215) 396-0390
www.chinmayapublications.com

Chinmaya Mission West
P.O. Box 129, Piercy, CA 95587, USA (707) 247-3488
www.chinmayamission.org

Central Chinmaya Mission Trust
Sandeepany Sadhanalaya
Saki Vihar Road
Mumbai 400 072, India
www.chinmayamission.com

Editorial Team
Editorial Advisors: Swami Shantananda & Swami Ishwarananda
Series Editors: Sadhna Sharma
Editorial Team: Ajay Marwaha, Jayanthi Balachander, Kamesh Pemmaraju,
Kreethi Venkat, Prabha Sriram, Radha Venkatraman, Rashmi Mehrotra,
Renu Prasad, Sanjay Pol & Vidya Ramraj
Permissions: Sinduja Kosgi
Layout: Sadhna Sharma
Book cover design & graphics: Sadhna Sharma
Images: Sadhna & Vidya Ramraj
Production Manager & Distribution: Lalet Sharma

Library of Congress Control Number: 2022917466
ISBN: 978-1-608-27032-3 Printed in the United States of America

Contents

PART FOUR
RELATIONSHIP WITH THE WORLD

Preface

The original concept of this topic arose from the many questions that the young people asked Swami Tejomayananda, while he lectured throughout the world. Wherever he went the same questions about family, school, dating, and work were on the minds of the youth. Observing this phenomenon, Swamiji out of his love and compassion, suggested that the Mananam team publish an issue that addresses their interests and concerns.

Although the concerns remain the same, challenges that young people face have changed with time. Now they have to face the consequences of the pandemic and global warming. This revised edition has been adapted to incorporate the concerns of young people accordingly. We hope that both youth and parents will benefit from the inspirational and practical writings of the authors in this book.

A whole section called 'Rising Above Challenges' has been added that covers practical solutions – to be practiced in day-to-day situations. Perhaps more than any other generation, today's young adults recognize the need to balance their work and family relationships and find it most challenging in the competitive work environment. In these pages, different authors describe how to bring about harmony and balance in life through proper relationships and right understanding. They explain how having the right relationship with oneself, family and friends, and the world leads to a life full of enthusiasm, success, and peace.

The Editors

> *What Youth require is a clear vision of a goal in life and exercises for the cultivation of the right values of life which alone can equip them to face the challenges of life with a smile.*
>
> *– Swami Chinmayananda*

Introduction:
The Successful Youth

Swami Tejomayananda

Our scriptures define an ideal youth as not only being of a certain age, but also as someone in whom you find the virtues of goodness and nobility. They list the physical, mental, and intellectual attributes needed to be an ideal youth and affirm that one who has these qualities and the resourcefulness to make use of them will have a fuller and happier life.

True abiding success is that in which steady inner growth and firm and abiding spiritual values (dharma) result in the welfare, well being, and prosperity of all people. When all are happy, then our happiness is automatically included. When we strive selfishly for only our own happiness, we can make many people miserable.

We must have a comprehensive vision of life. This vision has to be characterized by the welfare of all beings. Even though we have to live life day-to-day, event-to-event, and project-to-project, we need to constantly maintain the total vision.

There are three kinds of visions of life and they depend upon the condition of our minds.

1. Sattvika – Pure vision, ability to see oneness of all.
2. Rajasika – impure, governed by likes and dislikes.
3. Tamasika – dull and dark, fanatic and angry.

Only when your vision is one that serves society through your chosen path will there be an abiding success that blesses all of humanity, including yourself.

The Six A's of Success

1. Aptitude: A natural ability or interest in a particular field, such as music, arts, sports, and so forth. When you have a strong interest coupled with natural ability, you will enjoy what you do and can easily concentrate your mind to that activity.
2. Aspiration: A strong desire to achieve something high or great. This is a powerful mind force when coupled with aptitude.
3. Ability: Being able to perform skills physically and mentally. Skills may be acquired or may be natural.
4. Application: The act of applying one's mind and ability to a task. Being focused is a very important ingredient of success, whatever the chosen field.
5. Attitude: An emotion or mental feeling toward something, such as doing one's work. "When the going gets tough, the tough keep going."
6. Altar of dedication: Always seek a higher goal in life; devotees do everything for the Lord.

Success is not the final destination. Life is a journey – keep moving towards your higher goal. You may not always like what you get but accept it as a positive experience and move on. Some tasks may be boring but do them anyway with a positive attitude. Ultimately, you alone decide how you will act.

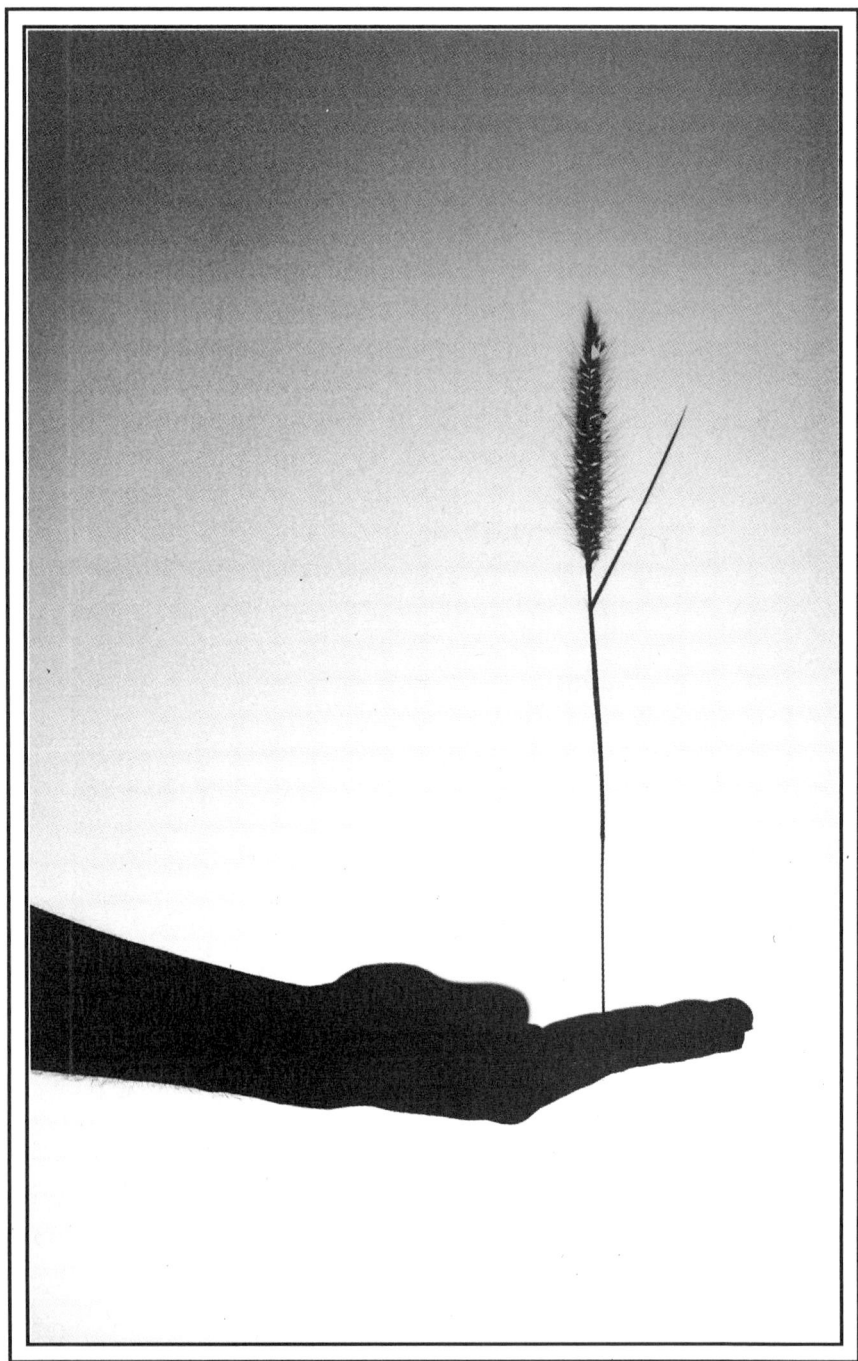

PART ONE
Relationship with Oneself

*"Cherish your visions and your dreams, as they
are the children of your soul, the blueprints of your
ultimate achievements."*

– Napoleon Hill

Strive for balance: Get things done – and have some fun. If you need to hit the books harder, do so; if you need to let yourself out of the library, come on out.

When you're little, your parents manage time for you. Now you're learning not just science, math, history, and English, but how to budget your time. How to fill your own afternoons and evenings and weekends? That's a biggie.

"How we spend our days is, of course, how we spend our lives" said writer Annie Dillard.

I spend a lot of my day staring at a computer screen and tapping at a keyboard. But I also make sure to get a little sunshine, and I try to get to the gym, or a movie, museum, or friend's home when possible. I meet my deadlines, but I also say yes to diversions. And if that sometimes means playing poker or watching reruns of Friends with friends, that's not wasted time. That's time well-spent..

Work and play – both. ...

Carol Weston

For Teens Only

3

1.

Learning to Love Yourself

Chérie Carter-Scott

At its core, loving yourself simply means believing in your own essential worthiness. It is nurturing a healthy sense of positive self-regard and knowing in your heart that you are a valuable link in the universal chain. Loving yourself also means actively caring for every facet of yourself. It shows up in every action you take, from putting on a sweater to protect yourself from a chill to leaving a job that does not fulfill you. It means tuning in to your own wants and needs and honoring them the exact same way you want your partner to attend to you.

Not everyone grows up to have an innate sense of high self-esteem or worthiness. In fact, most of us need to work at it to some degree throughout our lifetimes. Each person feels insufficient in one or more areas, whether physical, intellectual, financial, or in interpersonal dynamics, emotional maturity, or spiritual growth. However, respecting, nurturing, honoring, and cherishing yourself is your birthright and something you can learn.

> *At its core, loving yourself simply means believing in your own essential worthiness.*

Loving yourself is the best way to learn 'how' to love. Love is an action that requires certain understandings, skills,

4

and capacities. By practicing loving with yourself, you train yourself to advance to the next level – loving another.

Only when you have successfully mastered taking care of your own needs can you know how to extend that same attention to others. When you respect the validity of your own thoughts and feelings, you can apply that consideration to others. When you believe within yourself how valuable

> *It is only when you operate from the basis of being a whole person that you can find love based on want and not on need.*

you are, you can then bestow authentic affection on a partner.

If your objective is to play the game of love to win, then learning self-love is the first step you must take. Before you can roll the dice or even place your playing piece on the board, you need to tap into the inner reaches of your heart and soul and discover all that you are worth.

Being a Whole Person

Love can do many things for you: it can bring you joy, help you grow, and expand you in ways you never imagined possible. Yet one thing love can never do is make you whole. You are the only one who can make yourself complete.

Many people have bought into the myth that there is someone out there who will serve as our 'better half'. This paradigm presumes that we are incomplete and require a partner to make us whole, and it feeds into what I call the 'hole in the soul syndrome' – a core sense of insufficiency leading to feelings of emptiness, neediness, and self-reproach. Because of these feelings, we look for a partner to fill in the holes.

The grand irony is that the very sense of neediness that drives us to seek out love is exactly what will impede love from blossoming. Authentic love is attracted by those who desire it and is repelled by those who need it. Wanting connotes sufficiency and desire; needing connotes insufficiency and dependency. I 'need' creates a vacuum effect that forces you to clutch, grab, cling, and consume; I 'want' creates an openness that enables you to explore, consider, and shape the relationship you desire. It is only when you operate from the basis of being a whole person that you can find love based on 'want' and not on 'need'.

> *No matter how much adoration, attention, and emotional support someone gives you, you will always need more – and more and more – because the love you receive from another can never replace the love you need to give yourself.*

Victoria was raised in a household rich in luxury but devoid of affection. Her father was a very successful international business mogul who spent most of his time flying from one meeting to another, while her mother was preoccupied with her various charity events and social engagements. As a child, Victoria deeply longed for someone to notice her and lavish her with the attention she craved. She spent long hours alone in her bedroom, constructing elaborate fantasies about a famous musician who would write beautiful ballads declaring his undying love for her. She dreamed he would marry her and rescue her from her loneliness. She thought that once she found her beloved, she would no longer feel so empty inside and finally be happy.

As an adult, Victoria went from relationship to relationship, never able to find that idealized person who could quench her deep need for love. Her suitors stayed for brief periods but left with the same complaint: nothing they did ever seemed to be enough. Victoria was trapped in a cycle of seeking others to fill the hole in her soul. She became like an endless pit, insatiably draining her partners of their energy and vitality until they finally left, depleted. She would then immediately seek out another unsuspecting soul with whom she could repeat her pattern.

If you have personal development work to do in the area of self-love, as Victoria did, finding someone to love you is like trying to fill up a tank that has a hole in the bottom. No one can ever completely fill you up, because the leak will always create more need. No matter how much adoration, attention, and emotional support someone gives you, you will always need more – and more and more – because the love you receive from another can never replace the love you need to give yourself.

Questions for Self-Reflection:
1. Is self-love natural to me? How do I nurture and connect with myself on a daily basis?

2. Is my worthiness based on external validation? What steps can I take today to start practicing self-love?

3. How can one fuel self-love by tending to mental, emotional, physical and spiritual needs?

Coming up Next:

Studies have shown that what I say to myself has the same effect on my psychology as what others say about me. Just as others can build me up or demoralize me, so can I do the same for myself! Let us learn to use self-talk to improve and grow with the next article by Kimberley Kirberger.

2.

Sweeten Your Self-Talk

Kimberley Kirberger

I'm such a loser. I can't believe I said that. I look so fat
in these pants. He would never go out with someone
like me. Why can't I look like her? I can't do anything
right. Everyone else has it so much easier than I do.
What is wrong with me, anyway?

Does any of this sound familiar to you? If you were to actually
write down every negative thing you say to yourself in a day,
you would be shocked. Have you ever wondered why you say
such cruel things to yourself?

A lot of it comes from habit. Your mind repeats the
negative things that may have been said to you by teachers,
parents, or siblings. For instance, I grew up with three
older brothers. We used to say some pretty mean stuff to
one another. One of their favorite mean things to say to me
was, "Nobody likes you." They certainly never intended to
program a negative self-image into the mind of their beloved
sister – this is just one of the things siblings do. But things
people say to you can become part of your thinking, without
you even realizing it. This is why it is so important to begin
paying attention to your thoughts and becoming aware of the
way you speak to yourself.

Thoughts you have about yourself are called self-talk.
Positive thoughts about yourself are called positive self-talk.

Negative thoughts about yourself are called negative self-talk. Get into the habit of practicing positive self-talk whenever you have a few minutes alone. Remind yourself of compliments you have received in the past. Then think about what you like about you. What compliment would you give yourself? When you say nice things to yourself, it has the same effect as when others say kind things to you. Your feelings about yourself become more positive, you feel happier, and your self-confidence is boosted.

> *Thinking bad thoughts about yourself will make you feel bad.*
>
> *Thinking good thoughts about yourself will make you feel good. It's that simple.*

When you are lying in bed at night, get into the habit of going over your day and remembering the things you did that you feel good about. What did you do that you are proud of? Think about the small things - they count a lot. Every time your mind wanders to something negative, try to bring your focus back to the positive. At first you may find this difficult, but as you keep doing it, it gets easier.

You may worry that thinking positive thoughts about yourself will make you conceited. That won't happen. There's a big difference between thinking you're a good person and thinking you're the best person around. And even though this should never be the motivating factor, it doesn't hurt to consider who other people will be more attracted to: someone who is confident and secure, or someone who is constantly thinking about how stupid she is.

Thinking bad thoughts about yourself will make you feel bad. Thinking good thoughts about yourself will make you feel good. It's that simple. Sweetening your self-talk takes time. But as you practice saying kind things to yourself, your self-acceptance will grow.

Questions for Self-Reflection:
1. Will positive thinking make me conceited?

2. Why is it important to have self-acceptance?

3. Are people more attracted to others who are confident and secure, or to those who are preoccupied and worry about being a failure? Why?

Coming up Next:

In the thought-provoking article 'Keeping Your Life In Balance', author Harold L. Taylor questions if we are truly prioritizing the right experiences in life. He then provides wise observations on the cost of focusing on money alone and the opportunity cost of time outside of work.

"Your aim is yours, so don't change it for others."
– Swami Vivekananda.

3.

Keep Your Life in Balance

Harold L. Taylor

Keep your job – and your life – in perspective. With so much emphasis on success and achievement it sometimes becomes difficult to relax and enjoy life. Don't set your sights too high. Do the best you can, but don't kill yourself. Job burnout is a result of too much stress, and most jobs are stressful enough without adding your own unrealistic goals and expectations.

Set realistic goals. And realize that you can't do everything. Work on priorities – the twenty percent of the activities, which will bring you eighty percent of the results.

And always have some way of working off mental and emotional stress. Engage in a regular exercise program. Have interests other than your job. Make it a habit to talk over your problems with a close friend.

Above all, remember that what you 'are' is more important than what you 'do'.

It's possible that you work harder and faster under the pressure of unrealistic deadlines, but it's doubtful that you work better. Excellence does not come from tired, harried people. Mediocrity does. You would hate to have your plane piloted by someone who had been flying steadily for twelve hours. And you probably wouldn't feel too comfortable in a taxi if the driver had been driving all night. It's a fact that tired workers cause accidents. For the same reason, most skiing mishaps take place during that 'one last run'.

Don't talk yourself into believing that working steadily with your nose to the grindstone will lead to success. It will only lead to a flat nose. Work smarter, not harder. Concentrate on the goals you set for yourself. Every day do something to bring yourself closer to them. But recognize that you will have to ignore some of those unimportant activities that produce minimal results. You can't do everything and still keep your life in balance.

Many managers, particularly entrepreneurs, keep putting off their vacations; in some cases skipping them altogether. This is a mistake. Vacations should be blocked off in your calendar ahead of anything else. Relaxation is necessary in order to keep your mind alert, your body healthy, and your family together.

Some managers take better care of their office equipment and plant machinery than they do their own bodies. The human body is a lot more valuable than a hunk of machinery, and with a little care it may have a longer life. But one thing it doesn't have is a warranty or money-back guarantee. There are no returns or allowances. So spend all the time and money necessary for preventive maintenance.

> *Don't talk yourself into believing that working steadily with your nose to the grindstone will lead to success. It will only lead to a flat nose.*

To prevent yourself from filling your planning calendar with only work-related activities, schedule blocks of leisure time – those outings with the children, that movie with your spouse, that tennis game or shopping trip. Schedule them in ink, not pencil; make them definite, not tentative. Most people schedule them with the idea that they will go through with it 'if something more important doesn't come up'. And the 'something more important' is usually job related, and usually involves value in terms of dollars and cents.

Recognize that leisure time has value too. Not in terms of measurable 'dollars and cents', but in terms of long-term effectiveness; in terms of family accord and happiness; in terms of physical health and mental alertness. And in terms of success.

Some of us are guilty of neglecting our home life and giving top priority to our vocation-oriented activities. And we mean well. After all, our career is our bread and butter. It puts food on the table, a roof over our heads, and a car or two in the garage. And the more money we earn, the more tangibles we are able to give to our family and friends – tokens of our love and friendship.

But they're only tokens. If you're interested in giving a costly, yet valuable, gift to someone close to you, consider giving him or her some of your time. It's your most precious possession. You'll be giving them a piece of your life. How could you be more generous than that?

Material gifts are soon forgotten. But the gift of time is never forgotten. It's ironic that some of us spend our time in the pursuit of money and material possessions to give our loved ones. And in so doing, we deprive them of the very thing they want most, our time.

It's too often true that we always have time to attend a friend's funeral, but never had the time to visit him while he was alive.

Surveys have shown that the average workweek of executives is about sixty hours. Lunch hours, evenings, and weekends are used for business-related activities. Perhaps some executives can put in these kinds of hours and still lead a balanced life, but if you're included in this category ask yourself a few questions. Are you forming a work habit that hinders your willingness to delegate to others? Do you find that all this work is leading to exhaustion? Is your retention of information decreased as the work period is increased? Are you depriving yourself of time for self-renewal and creativity? It could be that you are increasing your hours but decreasing your effectiveness.

Don't believe that your income will vary directly with the number of hours you put in. That's a myth. It's what you put into those hours that makes the difference. Get organized and manage your time effectively, and you will accomplish more in eight hours than you did in twelve.

Exhibit A shows average distribution of time, assuming a person lives to be seventy years old. Does this approximate the way you spend your time? If so, ask yourself a few questions. Are the results you are achieving by watching TV worth eight years of your life? Are you fully utilizing that six years of travel time? How many of these seventy years include your family? Exhibit B shows the same breakdown in a pie chart form. There's not much time left for personal activities when you exclude your career and sleep. How are you spending the precious piece of personal time that's left after the other essentials such as eating, dressing, illness are also excluded? Is the career section expanding to wipe out most of this personal time?

There's only one way of preventing your career from wiping out the rest of your life,

Exhibit A		
An average life distribution of time		
Sleep	23 yrs.	32.9%
Work	16 yrs.	22.8%
TV	8 yrs.	11.4%
Leisure	4 ½yrs.	6.5%
Eating	6 yrs.	8.6%
Travel	6 yrs.	8.6%
Illness	4 yrs.	5.7%
Dressing	2 yrs.	2.8%
Religion	½ yr.	0.7%
Total	70 yrs.	100.0%

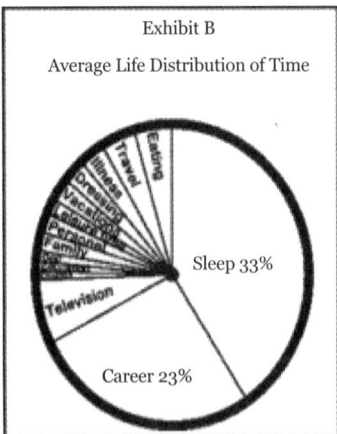

Exhibit B
Average Life Distribution of Time

Exhibit C
Balanced Life Distribution of
Time

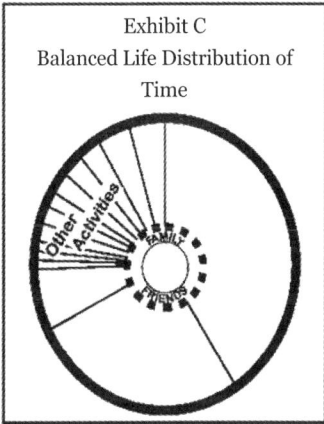

and that's by scheduling your meaningful activities into your planning diary and forcing your career to flow around these protected 'islands' of time. This is depicted in Exhibit C. Put whatever is important to you in the center of your life and protect it from the demands of your career and other people.

Time is life. Don't waste it on trivial matters. Use it for those priorities that are meaningful to 'you'.

Questions for Self-Reflection:
1. Is it true that working longer and longer hours always leads to higher productivity and more income? How can you improve your professional effectiveness?

2. People often refer to 'work life balance'. If you have only a limited amount of time, is it really possible to dedicate enough time to be successful with both work and life simultaneously?

Coming up Next:

In the next article Caroline Castrillon writes about ' Why a Growth Mindset Is Essential For Career Success' by first comparing it to a 'fixed mindset'. Then she discusses five ways that one can take control of one's mental attitude to foster a growth mindset.

4.

Why a Growth Mindset is Essential for Career Success

Caroline Castrillon

Mindset is everything. Whether you're talking about career success, starting your own business, getting through a tough workout or being a parent, having the right mindset can make the difference between success and failure. The concept of mindset can't be discussed without mentioning Carol Dweck and her insightful book, *Mindset: The New Psychology of Success.* After decades of research, world-renowned Stanford University psychologist Carol S. Dweck discovered the power of mindset. In her book, she outlines the differences between a fixed and growth mindset – showing how success in almost every area of life can be influenced by how we think about our talents and abilities. Once we harness the power of a growth mentality, studies show that it can be essential for career success.

Fixed vs. Growth Mindset

A fixed mindset assumes that our intelligence, character and creative ability are static. Basically, you are dealt a hand in life and are required to accept it. Believing that your qualities are set in stone creates a desire to prove yourself over and over again. A fixed mindset can result in career stagnation.

On the other hand, a growth mindset is based on the

idea that your essential qualities are things you can cultivate through your efforts. It assumes that everyone can change and grow through experience and practice. A growth mentality sees failure not as a detriment, but as a springboard to success. Failing is actually a form of learning. In one study conducted by Dweck with children, she offered four-year-olds a choice. They could either redo an easy jigsaw puzzle or try a harder one. Those with a fixed mindset chose the easier puzzles that would affirm their existing ability. They wanted to make sure they succeeded

> *A growth mentality sees failure not as a detriment, but as a springboard to success.*

to seem smart. The children with a growth mindset tried to stretch themselves because their definition of success was about becoming smarter. In her book, Dweck writes, "After thirty years, my research has shown that the view you adopt for yourself profoundly affects the way you lead your life. It can determine whether you become the person you want to be and whether you accomplish the things you value."

Developing a Growth Mindset

Mindset stems from our own set of powerful beliefs. A growth mentality assumes that views can be changed when they no longer allow us to achieve our goals. Here are five ways you can take control of your mental attitude to foster a growth mindset:

1. Embrace Failure

Fostering a growth mentality involves viewing failure as a positive rather than a negative. Everyone has setbacks. The key is to learn from each one and improve your decision making. Wildly successful people typically fail their way to success. Steven Spielberg was rejected from film school three times before getting his big break. Even Oprah Winfrey was fired from her news co-anchor position at a Baltimore TV station before going on to build a successful daytime talk show. A producer reportedly told her that she was "unfit for television news." Oprah later said, "I had no idea what I was in for or that this was going to be the greatest growing period of my adult life."

2. Become a Lifelong Learner

People with a growth mindset actively seek learning opportunities which result in more career success. Be curious about everything. Research shows that, while less successful people read mostly for entertainment, those at the top are avid readers of self-improvement books. In fact, 85% of successful people read two or more self-improvement or educational books per month. Another study revealed that 30% of executives said having a willingness to keep learning is the characteristic they consider most necessary for an employee to succeed.

> *Mindset stems from our own set of powerful beliefs.*

3. Seek Out Challenge

Challenges are opportunities that propel you forward towards your goals and help you grow. According to C.S. Lewis, "Hardships often prepare ordinary people for an extraordinary destiny." Don't underestimate the power of being able to overcome obstacles. Are you feeling too comfortable in your current career? That may be an indication that it's time to seek out new challenges. After all, the magic happens outside your comfort zone.

4. Go Beyond Your Limits

Another way to foster a growth mentality is to push yourself beyond what you think you can do. In one interesting study, researchers asked participants to cycle as hard as they could for 4,000 meters. Later, participants were given the same instructions but were able to race against an avatar of their previous ride. What they didn't know was that the avatar was going faster than they did previously. The result was that participants rode alongside their avatar, going significantly further than they did the first time. When you push yourself, you can surpass even your own expectations.

5. Ask For Feedback

People who want to grow personally and professionally tend to ask for and value feedback. This is because growth-oriented individuals are interested in developing and challenging themselves. They aren't afraid to be criticized or judged. Once you understand that you are responsible for your own growth, you will have the confidence to ask for feedback and learn from it.

A Changing World

With technology and business models changing rapidly, embracing a growth mindset is vital to career success. Workers will need to continuously learn new skills to remain competitive as automation technologies, including artificial intelligence, become more prevalent. According to a report by McKinsey, up to 375 million workers worldwide will need to change roles or learn new skills by 2030. Research shows that your mindset predicts achievement. It's not how good you are but how good you want to be that matters.

Questions for Self-Reflection:
1. How do you respond to 'constructive criticism'?

2. How do you act toward others? Are you a fixed-mindset person, focused on being smarter than others? Or, do you take advantage of the learning opportunities available to you through your peers?

Coming up Next:

Ancient yogic and ayurvedic practices are time-tested means to achieving radiant good health. From Hatha yoga and pranayama, to tips on following a healthy diet, and enjoying relaxing sleep, read Swami Jyotirmayananda's guide to all-round healthy living.

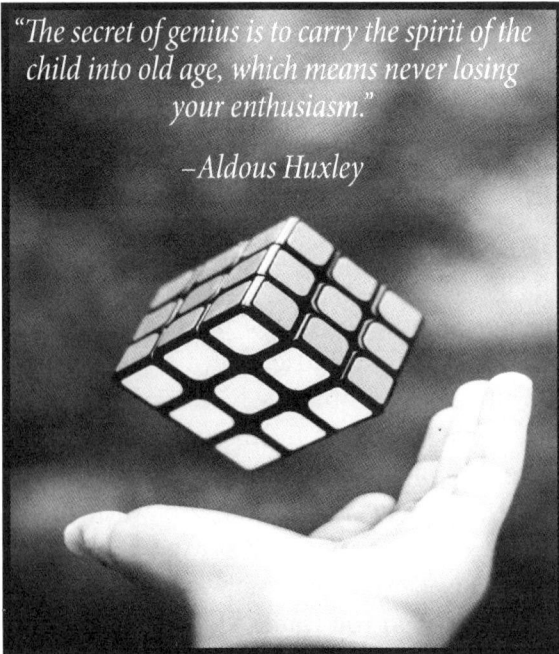

"The secret of genius is to carry the spirit of the child into old age, which means never losing your enthusiasm."

–Aldous Huxley

5.

Towards Radiant Health

Swami Jyotirmayananda

On Hatha Yoga

Hatha yoga is the world's most ancient system of physical and mental culture and it has been practiced by yogis in India for centuries. It is a marvelous system of psychophysical exercises. The poses (asanas) of hatha yoga are performed with mental serenity as well as physical poise and grace. They are meant to promote elasticity of the spine and health of the nervous system. Yoga exercises nourish the roots of the nerves with subtle prana or vital energy and are therefore, different from most systems of physical culture.

With the key of hatha yoga, you can unlock the infinite treasure of prana, regain lost health, acquire strength of mind, unfold hidden powers of the spirit, amass the wealth of willpower, attain success in every walk of life, and ascend to the mansion of Self-realization!

Prana

Prana is the subtlest form of energy. As the universal storehouse of energy, it underlies all physical energies such as electricity, magnetism, light, heat, and so on, and also sustains all mental processes such as thinking, feeling, willing, and reasoning.

Prana is the manifestation of the supreme Spirit as the sustainer of life and all forces in the world.

Due to prana, the ocean surges, the sun shines in the heavens, the stars move along their definite courses, and the earth and other planets revolve around the sun. Due to prana, the rivers flow towards the ocean and the mountains hold their heads high in the air. Without prana, there would be no life on earth. This is the meaning of prana in a broader sense.

> *With the key of hatha yoga, you can unlock the infinite treasure of prana, regain lost health, acquire strength of mind, unfold hidden powers of the spirit, amass the wealth of willpower, attain success in every walk of life, and ascend to the mansion of Self-realization!*

In a limited sense, prana is the vital force that sustains life by performing various vital functions that keep the body alive. Breathing is one such effect of prana. By controlling and harmonizing the breath, a yogi gains control over the subtle prana, which is linked to the mind and senses, which in turn, are linked to the soul.

Exercises in Breath Awareness

- Breathe in an effortless natural way and watch your breath. Feel that with each breath you are drawing cosmic energy from the ocean of universal life. This inhaled energy or prana is permeating every fiber of your being, every vein and artery, every nerve and cell of your body. With each exhalation, feel that all the toxins from your body and all the complexes of your mind are being expelled. Gradually you are being attuned with the ocean of universal life.
- As you watch your normal breathing in an effortless way, feel your body absorbing energy through

respiration. As the breath enters your lungs, feel that your body is like the ocean shore, receiving the tide upon its sandy beach. Like the beach, your body is exhilarated by the touch of the universal ocean of prana. Then with the outgoing breath, feel that the tide is turning back, leaving the sandy shore – and your body – refreshed. Your body is thus bathed and refreshed at every moment by the surfing ocean of universal prana.

- While breathing in, feel that a stream of Om, permeated by the Divine Presence, is entering through your nostrils. With each incoming breath, feel that your consciousness is expanding gradually to infinity and that you are dissolving your ego in the vast expansion of the Self. With each outgoing breath, feel that you are gradually coming back from infinite expansion and returning to individual consciousness.
- Gently, without interference, observe your breathing and mentally associate the Soham mantra with your breath. Feel that the incoming breath represents 'So' and the outgoing breath represent 'Ham'. 'So' means That, the Divine Self, which is beyond the mind, senses, and ego. 'Ham' means I am. Thus, Soham means 'That am I' and, with every breath you take, you are asserting your oneness with God, the Divine Self.

The Value of a Vegetarian Diet

Pure food makes your body healthy and full of vitality, and helps keep your mind calm, balanced, and peaceful. Vegetarian food is purer than non-vegetarian food, and therefore, provides many benefits for body and mind. Furthermore, the human body is not well designed to receive nutrition from meat. Nutrition is assimilated more efficiently from a vegetarian diet.

Non-vegetarian food is risky for your health because so many artificial substances are given to commercially raised animals. By eating meat, you are increasing the level of toxins in your body.

You also never know what diseases were present or about to develop in the animals' body when it was killed. These diseases may not be detected when the meat is inspected according to usual standards. There is a humorous anecdote about a man who was being served dinner at a party. When the meat was offered to him he declined saying, "I will have everything else you have, not the meat." "Why, have you become vegetarian?" The host asked. "Oh no," he replied, "I am a meat inspector and, therefore I know the quality of that meat and where it came from."

> *Non-vegetarian food is risky for your health because so many artificial substances are given to commercially raised animals.*

Being a vegetarian also helps you to maintain a more joyous and elevated state of mind. When you eat meat, one part of your mind knows how the animal was brought to the slaughterhouse and killed, how its entrails were removed and how it was cut up. However, one never wants to think about these things, especially while eating the meat.

Life is very dear to all animals. When an animal is killed, it experiences great fear, which is recorded in its body in a subtle way. So, when you later eat that animal, you are imbibing the impressions of that fright.

A carefully planned vegetarian diet, therefore, helps keep the body free of toxins and, most important of all, keeps the sensitive mind free of the subtle negative impressions that are generated by the killing of animals. If you are eating non-vegetarian food, you would benefit greatly by gradually moving away from it and beginning to enjoy more nourishing vegetarian food that can be prepared in the most delightful and flavorful ways.

Enjoying the Gift of Sleep

Healthy sleep is a great attainment. It is a sign of physical as well as psychological health. If your personality is highly integrated you can control sleep and sleep at will.

Sleep is necessary so that the physical body can rest and recharge itself at the end of each day. During sleep, special physiological and chemical changes occur in the body. Your blood becomes more alkaline and nature works to expel toxins or poisons. Your tired body heals itself faster during sleep because your mind and ego do not interfere at that time.

Sleep is a great aid in securing health, in promoting physical and mental balance, and in curing disease. In every way, it is a marvelous divine medicine, given as a gift by nature.

Physical Hints for Promoting Healthy Sleep

Here are some hints, if followed, will enable one to sleep healthily:

- Do not depend on stimulants to keep awake or sleeping pills to go to sleep. Let sleep emerge naturally from your heart and bathe your body in fresh energy. The sleep produced under the influence of drugs is not as healing as natural sleep. These drugs depress your nerves, and your mind becomes duller and duller as time passes by.
- Practice hatha yoga's powerful exercises to promote flexibility and strength of the body, deep and complete breathing, and profound relaxation. These exercises recharge your physical body with

prana (vital energy). As you continue doing them with regularity and precision, you will enjoy healthier sleep.

- Follow a sensible diet and eat in moderation, allowing adequate time for good digestion. Diet plays a great part in soothing your nerves and promoting a restful sleep. As a rule, do not take heavy food before going to sleep. In the Ashram in India, the evening meal is served at or before sunset so that there is sufficient time for the food to be digested before the students go to sleep.
- Sleeping on your left side also helps to promote better sleep. This encourages the breath to flow through the right nostril, aiding in the assimilation and digestion of food, as well as providing other benefits to the body while it sleeps.
- Do not sleep with your head toward the north. To do so allows the polar magnetic pull to interfere with the functioning of your brain.
- A good principle to follow is, "Early to bed, early to rise." Set a definite time for going to sleep that utilizes your best energies and try to maintain it.
- Practice moderation in sleeping, eating, playing, studying, meditating, and in all aspects of your life. Too much or too little of anything can put stress on your nerves and misbalance your psychophysical personality.

Elevate Your Mind

Before going to sleep, try to elevate your mind. Read some elevating passages from an inspiring book, pray with a sincere heart, or repeat a mantra (a divine name) with feeling and devotion. The suggestions that you give to your mind before sleeping are carried to your unconscious in a spontaneous manner and they continue to operate during the night. Even if you read or pray for only five minutes, that effort educates your unconscious profoundly.

If you know the art of repeating mantra or the Divine names (such as OM, Shri Ram, Krishna, Jesus and others) with devotional feeling, you do not need any other form of lullaby. With each repetition, feel you are surrendering yourself to God, who is the embodiment of love and sweetness. In this way, repetition of mantra gently rocks you to sleep, free of care and anxiety.

> *If your personality is highly integrated you can control sleep and sleep at will.*

Repetition of the mantra, Om Namo Narayana, is a special yogic sleeping potion! According to Hindu mythology, the greatest sleeper in the world is God in the form of Lord Narayana, who constantly sleeps on the couch of the Shesha serpent. In the twinkling of an eye, He creates the world and dissolves it but, unconcerned by all this, He continues to enjoy infinite peace and bliss. If you were to realize that Lord Narayana, the Divine Self, as the Reality within you, you too could experience the sleep of supreme peace at every moment.

You sleep most profoundly when your mind is awake to the higher Reality within, when you realize that your personality is a wave in the cosmic ocean of life, sustained with infinite compassion by Divine will. When you discover that you do not carry the strings of your personality in your own hands, but, rather, you are ever in Divine Hands, you can easily allow your nerves to relax and carry you into deep, healthy sleep.

Questions for Self-Reflection:
1. Why is good health important for a spiritual seeker?

2 . What can I do to get a good night's sleep?

3. Do you think following a vegetarian diet is a better option than a non-vegetarian one?

Coming up Next:

In the next article "Can I Care About How I Look – and Still Be Spiritual?", the author, Nasim Mansuri, draws from the teachings of her Baha'i faith to answer this question.

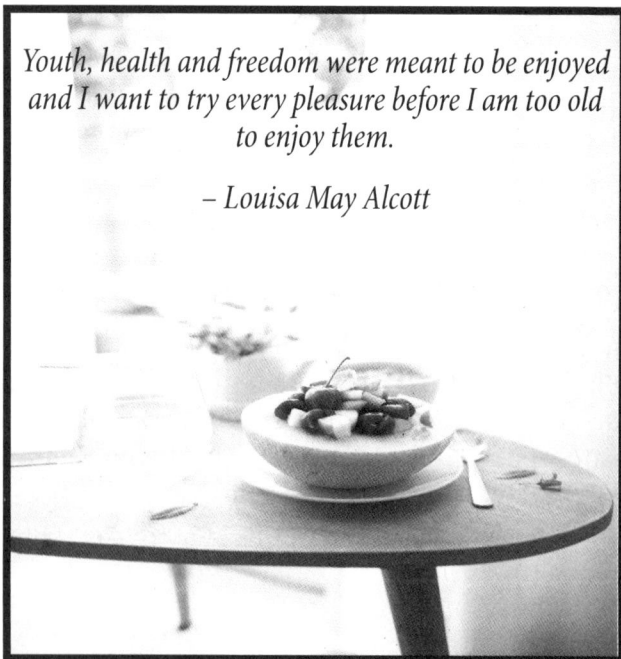

Youth, health and freedom were meant to be enjoyed and I want to try every pleasure before I am too old to enjoy them.

– Louisa May Alcott

6.

Can I Care about How I Look – and Still be Spiritual?

Nasim Mansuri

Is it vain to care about your appearance – or could it be just another way of being spiritual?

When we consider vanity, we generally think of focusing primarily on how we look physically – and when we think of spirituality, it usually refers to a deeper, more profound condition of the soul, one that goes beyond the mere physical. The two terms can seem, then, like opposites.

Our mental image of a pure, good person, one more in touch with the spiritual and the divine, tends to be someone with few possessions, sitting in the dust and dressed in rags while praying fervently – so elevated above the material world that they have no need to pay it any attention.

That image of detached spirituality clashes directly with the ideals of beauty society demands we follow. As a young girl, I felt constantly bombarded with different beauty ideals, most of them involving some product or another: makeup, clothes, shoes, perfume. Even in the most isolated places, young people feel the pressure to look perfect, and the definition of 'perfect' always changes with the dictates of style and fashion.

But the same society tells us, especially as girls, to avoid vanity. The kind of girl who cares too much about her appearance, looks too good in selfies and spends too much time getting ready, we're told, is shallow, self-centered and mean. Being 'good', then, seems to imply paying little attention to one's appearance, so as to not appear vain.

What a confusing dichotomy – and one in which too many girls end up feeling caught. How do we satisfy society's impossibly high expectations of our appearance, while also remaining spiritual, humble and unconcerned?

For a long time, I felt a little guilty whenever I indulged in buying a nice perfume, or spent too much time doing my hair or clothes. I thought I was wasting time being vain.

But it turns out, from my understanding of the Baha'i teachings, that caring about your appearance does not necessarily equal vanity. In fact, the Baha'i teachings say this:

> "Therefore strive that the greatest cleanliness and sanctity … should be resplendent among the Baha'is, and that the companions of God should surpass the rest of mankind in all conditions and perfections; that they may be physically and morally superior to others; that through cleanliness and purity, refinement and health, they may be the chief of wise men, and that by their enfranchisement, their prudence, and the control of their desires, they may be the princes of the pure, the free and the wise.
> – Abdu'l-Baha, Baha'i World Faith"

This kind of superiority doesn't preclude humility, of course – that's the moral part. But Abdu'l-Baha says that we should aspire to physical perfection as well as moral perfection. He encouraged us to have some concern about our appearance, our cleanliness, our 'enfranchisement; – which means freedom from dependence or addiction of any kind.

So what does physical perfection look like? For hundreds of years, people have decked out churches and temples in gold and other riches for the sake of beauty, and in the name of consumerism and the pursuit of physical attractiveness, we continue to pile expensive products on our bodies. We all too easily associate luxury with beauty, which turns beauty into a decidedly material thing: a potential cause of disunity or shame, solely associated with money and power. We also

> *So what about beauty that doesn't depend on luxury? From a Baha'i perspective, we achieve optimal physical beauty not through vanity, but through purity, simplicity and cleanliness*

know, from the Baha'i writings, never to place spiritual value on mere objects:

"Our greatest efforts must be directed towards detachment from the things of the world; we must strive to become more spiritual, more luminous, to follow the counsel of the Divine Teaching, to serve the cause of unity and true equality, to be merciful, to reflect the love of the Highest on all men, so that the light of the Spirit shall be apparent in all our deeds ..."
– Abdu'l-Baha, Paris Talks

So what about beauty that doesn't depend on luxury? From a Baha'i perspective, we achieve optimal physical beauty not through vanity, but through purity, simplicity and cleanliness. In the most holy book of the Baha'i Faith, Baha'u'llah advised us "To be the essence of cleanliness." – p. 50. That Baha'i law includes bathing regularly, wearing clean clothes, trimming our nails, smelling pleasant, and "generally to be the essence of cleanliness and refinement." – Ibid., p. 236.

A person whose clothes are impeccable, who is clean all over, whose nails are nicely cut, who is perfumed – that sounds like an excellent definition of beauty, and one that doesn't depend on luxury or vanity. Anyone can achieve this, even those who have the most meagre of means.

With our hectic lives – especially if you're a college student like me in a place with no dress code – being 100% clean and neat all the time requires some effort. It's easy to throw on clothes haphazardly, to continuously postpone doing my nails, to purposefully ignore a stain on a jacket for the sake of convenience. But what does that say about us, and what effect does it have on our souls?

> *By caring for our physical appearance and cleanliness, we're also caring for our spiritual health. Our body and our soul reflect one another in this respect.*

Abdu'l-Baha spoke of the relationship between our cleanliness – and therefore our physical appearance – and our spirit:

> "Even in the physical realm, cleanliness will conduce to spirituality, as the Holy Writings clearly state. And although bodily cleanliness is a physical thing, it hath, nevertheless, a powerful influence on the life of the spirit … The purport is that physical cleanliness doth also exert its effect upon the human soul." – Abdu'l-Baha, Selections from the Writings of Abdu'l-Baha

By caring for our physical appearance and cleanliness, we're also caring for our spiritual health. Our body and our soul reflect one another in this respect. In reality, then, the dichotomy that forces us to choose between looking good and 'being' good doesn't really exist – they can build on each other.

While I can't say I reach this standard daily yet, I do feel a sense of inner peace when I'm completely clean, neat, fresh and organized. I used to think of that feeling as vanity, but I might have been wrong all along. Maybe that sense of freshness and peace can give us a healthy sign of our spiritual appreciation for beauty – one that will help us reach a higher level of perfection in our souls, as well:

> "Should a man wish to adorn himself with the ornaments of the earth, to wear its apparels, or partake of the benefits it can bestow, no harm can befall him, if he alloweth nothing whatever to intervene between him and God, for God hath ordained every good thing, whether created in the heavens or in the earth, for such of His servants as truly believe in Him. Eat ye, O people, of the good things which God hath allowed you, and deprive not yourselves from His wondrous bounties."
> –Baha'u'llah,
> Gleanings from the Writings of Baha'u'llah

Questions for Self-Reflection:
1. What is your understanding of the term 'inner beauty'? Is it different from 'outer beauty'? If so, how?

2. When you see someone well dressed and groomed, what feeling does that bring to you?.

Coming up Next:

In the article on vegetarianism, Swami Chinmayananda explains that a spiritual culture is essentially geared for the life of meditation, in which the mind should be calm and peaceful, which in turn requires that the food one eats should be devoid of toxins and easy to digest. Simple vegetarian food is the least toxic and best suited for this purpose.

7.

On Vegetarianism

Swami Chinmayananda

Q: Why is vegetarian food considered better in India?

A: Eat we must. What we like to eat depends upon one's taste. There are only four things available – stones, plants, animals, and humans. Unfortunately, we cannot eat stones because our system is not geared to digest and assimilate them directly. And even though we sometimes destroy human beings with our cruelty, our progressive culture does not allow eating them. That leaves us the vegetable and the animal kingdom to choose from. No doubt, since prehistoric times, animals have been eaten, but we find that the very first progenitor of humanity, Adam himself, was eating only vegetables. It is only his second son who started this easy method of obtaining food because agriculture seemed to be too difficult for him, as it required a continuous process of putting forward effort in order to produce. Whereas sitting behind a stone, waiting for innocent animals to come along, destroying and eating them seemed to be the easier way!

Q: How did the idea of vegetarianism develop in India?

A: We learned that vegetables can stay fresh up to forty-eight hours, but meat deteriorates and becomes harmful very quickly. Furthermore, within the human body, during the process of digestion, food remains in the digestive system for about forty-eight hours. Fruit and vegetables digest much faster than meat. Whatever stays longer in the intestines starts to decay with the heat of the body system, which creates a lot of toxins.

Let me explain this idea of toxicity a little more. You must have noticed that generally man eats only those animals that don't eat other animals. It is very difficult for man to digest and assimilate carnivorous animals. This suggests that they must be highly toxic to his system. It also suggests that a certain amount of toxicity is present in the first round of eaten animals, because twice removed the meat of carnivorous animals becomes impossible to eat!

Q: So, it seems that what one eats determines a trip to the doctor and remaining healthy. But in what way does vegetarian food help a person's mind? Did people discover that it affects the mental temperament?

A: The food that we take in and the thoughts and actions that spring forth from us have a distinct relationship. In the computer world, there is a well-known saying – garbage in, garbage out. This seems to be true of our bodies as well. If you put toxic food – garbage – into your system, in the long run the texture of your thoughts and actions have a tendency to become more unreconciling, extremely selfish, less concerned for others, and lusty, and therefore potentially dangerous to the social order.

Fruit and vegetables digest much faster than meat. Whatever stays longer in the intestines starts to decay with the heat of the body system, which creates a lot of toxins.

Thus, we can see that toxins in the system bring about a lot of mental disturbances. The same principle applies to drinking alcohol. Since our culture is essentially geared for the life of meditation, the mind that is constantly agitated and wandering finds it difficult to plunge into meditation. To such an individual, the toxin is an obstacle in reaching his goal. Probably this must have been the reason why the rishis in the jungles ate only fruits, roots, leaves, and water. Those who take non-vegetarian food may be very uncontrolled because of the toxins in their food. Watch a vegetarian and a non-vegetarian animal. All herbaceous animals are available for eating; whereas the non-vegetarian or carnivorous animals are never eaten, even by hard core non-vegetarians. Why is this? Because carnivorous animals have got so much toxicity in them that it means almost death to eat them.

> *The food that we take in and the thoughts and action that springs forth from us have a distinct relationship.*

Questions for Self-Reflection:

1. Why do we think we have the moral right to take away a life or cause pain and sorrow to animals for our eating pleasure?

2. Is the importance of life for animals any less than it is for us humans?

3. What is the environmental impact of the meat industry and how is it contributing to greenhouse gases, loss of forest cover, and inordinate water usage and pollution?

Coming up Next:

Eckhart Tolle discusses the creation of 'not self' – the ego and our identification with it, which alienates us from Consciousness – our own true self.

Take Care of the Body

Avoid overeating and select the food that agrees with you and is conducive to the harmony of the body. Many people think eating food is the greatest exercise for the stomach! That is not enough. Apart from eating healthy food, you must also have some exercise of all the limbs, especially some exercises of the stomach, so that your digestion, assimilation, and evacuation can be as good as possible.

These are the primary rules to be followed. Our ancient teachers said "The first duty is to take care of the body, which is the means for the pursuit of spiritual life." Sometimes weak persons come to me and say, "I want to forget my body!" What kind of body do they have? They are just a mass of skin and bones! Develop the body properly. You can never forget the body if it is not in a healthy condition.

– Swami Yatiswarananda
Meditation and Spiritual Life

8.

Conditioned by the Past: Karma and Consciousness

Eckhart Tolle

The voice in the head has a life of its own. Most people are at the mercy of that voice; they are possessed by thought, by the mind. And since the mind is conditioned by the past, you are then forced to reenact the past again and again.

The Eastern term for this is karma. When you are identified with that voice, you don't know this, of course. If you knew it, you would no longer be possessed because you are only truly possessed when you mistake the possessing entity for who you are, that is to say, when you become it.

For thousands of years, humanity has been increasingly mind-possessed, failing to recognize the possessing entity as 'not self.' Through complete identification with the mind, a false sense of self – the ego – came into existence. The density of the ego depends on the degree to which you – the consciousness – are identified with your mind, with thinking. Thinking is no more than a tiny aspect of the totality of consciousness, the totality of who you are.

The degree of identification with the mind differs from person to person. Some people enjoy periods of freedom from it, however brief, and the peace, joy, and aliveness they experience in those moments make life worth living. These are also the moments when creativity, love, and compassion arise.

Others are constantly trapped in the egoic state. They are

alienated from themselves, as well as from others, and the world around them. When you look at them, you may see the tension in their face, perhaps the furrowed brow, or the absent or staring expression in their eyes. Most of their attention is absorbed by thinking, and so they don't really see you, and they are not really listening to you. They are not present in any situation, their attention being either in the past or future which, of course, exist only in the mind as thought forms. Or they relate to you through some kind of role they play and so are not themselves. Most people are alienated from who they are, and some are alienated to such a degree that the way they behave and interact is recognized as 'phony' by almost everyone, except those who are equally phony, equally alienated from who they are.

> *Through complete identification with the mind, a false sense of self – the ego – came into existence.*

Alienation means you don't feel at ease in any situation, any place, or with any person, not even with yourself. You are always trying to get 'home' but never feel at home. Some of the greatest writers of the twentieth century, such as Franz Kafka, Albert Camus, T. S. Eliot, and James Joyce, recognized alienation as the universal dilemma of human existence, probably felt it deeply within themselves and so were able to express it brilliantly in their works. They don't offer a solution. Their contribution is to show us a reflection of the human predicament so that we can see it more clearly.

> *Alienation means you don't feel at ease in any situation, any place, or with any person, not even with yourself.*

To see one's predicament clearly is a first step toward going beyond it. So while you are perhaps still waiting for something significant to happen in your life, you may not realize that the

39

ECKHART TOLLE

most significant thing that can happen to a human being has already happened within you: the beginning of the separation process of thinking and awareness.

Questions for Self-Reflection:
1. If the present life is the result of past actions, is a person's life already predetermined?

2. To what degree are you identified with your mind or thinking?

3. What are your thought patterns? Are you able to separate thinking from awareness?

Coming up Next:

With his characteristic simplicity and deep wisdom, Swami Tejomayananda gives gems of advice to young adults who are on the verge of leaving their nests and finding their own wings to fly. What attitude should one adopt, which one should you avoid? Read this interview to get some practical tips on how to face life's challenges.

We are what our thoughts have made us; so take care about what you think. Words are secondary. Thoughts live; they travel far.

- Swami Vivekananda

9.

Interview with Swami Tejomayananda

Compiled by the Editors

Q: How can one cultivate focus at work without getting distracted by surrounding events?

A: If you are truly inspired by your work or job, then you will be totally absorbed in it, and things or events around will not distract you. So, most importantly, you have to find that work or job which truly inspires you. Also realize that someone else cannot live your life and you cannot live someone else's life. You must remind yourself of this and therefore commit yourself to taking charge of your life. This way you will remain focused.

Q: Sometimes people find something inspiring – something that they would love to do, but they don't get an opportunity to do it because they do not get that job, they do not get an opportunity to do it. What should a person in that situation do?

A: One can either be a master of circumstances or a victim of them. If one says that he has inspiration but has no opportunities, then that person is not sufficiently inspired. A truly inspired person will create the opportunities and charge ahead. I heard a joke recently that illustrates what I am saying. It is said that one must learn from Noah. He floated his company when the world was in liquidation!

Q: We do not know what exactly to do in life, everyone seems to be following a trend. Everybody wants to do an MBA, but nobody knows why they want to do it!

A: The problem of 'what to do' is not a new one. It has always been there in all ages. In our lives we notice that we have different interests at different stages. As a child we may have been interested in one particular thing, while we may get interested in something else when we enter college. For example, Swami Vivekananda as a boy was very much interested in becoming a Tangewala (carriage driver). However, his interests changed when he grew up. Similarly, we may at times feel like becoming a music director, and at other times becoming a professor, and so on. This is nothing new.

> *If you are determined enough, you will find that all support and guidance will automatically come to you.*

Q: In our life we have so many choices. How do we make the right choice?

A: You will notice that among all your interests, the subject in which you have an aptitude will fascinate you. You will find that interest in this subject overshadows all other interests and you are easily able to sacrifice other interests in its favor. The question of what to do will not bother you. Consistency and determination will automatically come. You will have to discover this for yourself.

Now suppose you are not able to find out what your real interests are, then what to do? Follow this simple technique: note down all your interests and just choose anyone of them. Once you have chosen a field, make it a point to develop interest and grow in it. In fact, you will find every subject interesting if you take interest in it!

Q: Parents just do not understand us, there is a big generation gap. They think we are not ambitious and too fun loving. They think we are not serious about anything and do not work hard enough.

A: Stop blaming your parents! When you were a child you can say that your parents were responsible for everything you do. It is they who decide which school you go to and so on.

But once you mature and go to college and university, you can no longer say that your parents are responsible for everything. It is not that your parents do not understand you. They will understand and support you provided you show consistency and results in whatever you do. Simply being adamant without any consistency, and changing your interest every now and then, will not serve any purpose.

Enough of putting the blame on somebody else. Take responsibility for your life and put it in your own hands. Start from wherever you are and show the results. Have faith in yourself. There is no need to have low self-esteem. If you are determined enough, you will find that all support and guidance will automatically come to you.

In all stages of life, everyone will face some obstacle or the other. There may be many who may criticize and discourage you. But hold on to your faith. If a task is worthy of doing, then do it. Do not get angry when a person criticizes you. If support does not come from one source, then it will come from another. Learn to enjoy your work and make the most of it. Do not let the fear of failure hold you back. If you are afraid of failing, you will never achieve anything. Now stop looking for excuses and sympathy, TAKE CHARGE OF YOUR OWN LIFE. You have to lift yourself up; do not depend on others to pull you up. Take charge and you will become successful.

Questions for Self-Reflection:
1. How can I discover what my real interest and aptitude in life is?

2. How can I keep up my resolve and self esteem in the face of criticism?

3. How can devotion help me have faith in myself?

Coming up Next:

The upcoming article by Vivek Gupta is about how to navigate challenges cheerfully and to have a Giving personality. To begin this process one has to direct oneself and engage in an 'Early Challenge'. Read on to know more about this challenge.

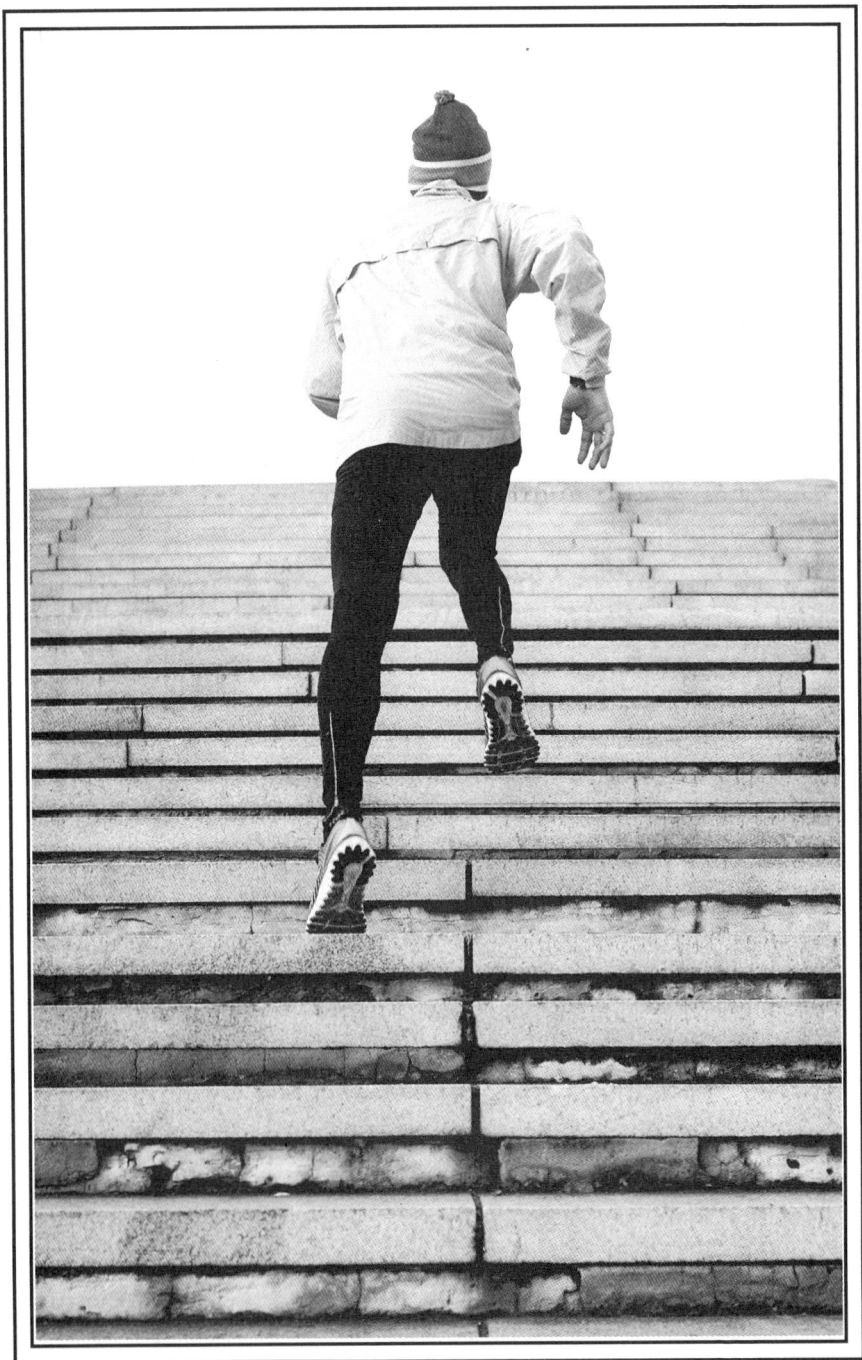

PART TWO

Rising Before Challenges

Q: Who is a karma yogi?

A: A karma yogi is a selfless worker who follows the path of action. He or she performs selfless activity, dedicating all his or her actions to a higher ideal and gives up all sense of doership.

– Swami Chinmayananda

When Benjamin Franklin was a boy, he divided his day and night into compartments of fifteen minutes each. Every hour had four compartments and twenty-four hours yielded ninty-six compartments. He then said, "So many compartments, I will devote to sleep, so many compartments, I will give by looking after the body. But, we must live a life of discipline.

So many compartments, I will give to eating, so many compartments I will give to studying. So many compartments, I will give to games ." He led a disciplined life as a boy. Benjamin Franklin did not waiver from the program he had fixed for himself. Our way may not be the way of Benjamin Franklin – this was just an example.

J.P. Vaswani

10.

Navigating Challenges Cheerfully

Vivek Gupta

With changes come challenges but the nature of living is change. Especially for young adults – changing hormones, changing dorms, changing relationships. Being young can be disorienting.

As children what caused us to be disoriented? If we recollect, it would be the playground equipment like a merry-go-round. We have to be clear though; the merry-go-round only caused disorientation if we held on to the equipment. For the kids just pushing or the kids just watching, there was no disorientation. Extend this example to nature of living, it is said that every facet of the multiverse is spinning. Ignoring this blatant fact, we 'hold on to this ride' causing us to become more disoriented. And what do we do to orient ourselves? Strangely, instead of letting go we 'hold on tighter!' The result of our decades of living in this manner is the reason for feeling directionless.

Almost every human feels incomplete. Those without any direction, project completion onto the world. IF I graduate from this College THEN I will be complete. IF my children listen to me THEN I will be complete. This thought process of projecting and depending is termed 'attachment'. Some may think, I am not attached! The inconspicuous test of attachment is being afraid. The conspicuous test of attachment is being angry. So are we attached?...Yes we are!

Complaining about how attractive the world is and criticizing how attached we are to this world is futile. This does not lead to growth. A growth mindset is one that is ever reflecting on how to be better and how to do better. Perhaps this thought process could be termed as 'passion'.

A successful strategy to detach is to practice a passion to give. Give your resources to charity. Give your time to the community. Give your effort to (self) capability. If you are a 'giving personality' you will naturally feel a sense of completeness by giving. Intellectually analyzing giving as a means to feeling complete will lead you to the conclusion that this is illogical and so ineffective. My experience has shown me giving is the means to grow out of insecurity and into independence. By giving, one can give away the longing for recognition, appreciation, even inclusion.

> *A growth mindset is one that is ever reflecting on how to be better and how to do better. Perhaps this thought process is passion.*

To be givers we need to be generators too. And this can be nurtured at a young age as an 'early personality trait'. With society's shift to living and working from home, there is more closeness and there can be more conflict. The cranky way to deal with the constant demands of familial responsibilities and community responsibilities is to 'fire-fight' or react. On the other hand, a cheerful way to tend to such diverse responsibilities is to 'rise-early' in other words respond to the situation.

A classical framework for contemplation in Vedanta is the Pancha-Kosha-Viveka-Dhyana. Sounds complicated! Simply put, contemplation is 'directing' our equipment rather than 'being controlled' by them. If we want to feel free unconditionally, then we have to practice contemplation unconditionally, not just in a controlled space at a controlled time.

VIVEK GUPTA

In an effort to master this kind of control Cleveland and Niagara Communities have engaged in the Early Challenge:

- Sleep EARLY – sleeping early encourages our body to be fresher
- Wake EARLY – waking early empowers our intellect to be clearer
- Study EARLY – studying early enables our mind to be purer
- Walk EARLY – walking early enlivens our breath to be deeper
- Sync EARLY – syncing early, in other words connecting, escorts our ego to be kinder

To navigate challenges cheerfully, one's general life direction should be towards being a 'Giving Personality' and our specific thought direction has to be towards being an 'Early Personality'.

Questions for Self-Reflection:
1. What am I attached to? Am I holding on tight to something?

2. What are my capabilities that I can give?

3. To become a giver and a director of my equipment, what will it take for me to engage in the 'Early Challenge'?

Coming up Next:

Fear is a natural and protective human instinct. But in many of us fear becomes a handicap that makes us anxious and unable to act in the world. Swami Purushottamananda explains some strategies for coping with and reducing our crippling fear.

11.

On Overcoming Fear

Swami Purushottamananda
(Ramakrishna Mission)

People might say, 'fear not' but a little thought reveals that fear is indispensable for our very existence. Are we not expected to be on guard against dangers from wicked people or wild beasts? For self-protection carefulness is inevitable; and this carefulness proceeds only from a sense of apprehension. Thus, essentially it is this fear that helps us protect ourselves. But fear turns into a real evil when we start fearing illogically – for example, conjuring up hideous things or remaining in a state of fear even after preparing well for exams, or becoming too nervous waiting for the results. Then there are many young people who yield to stage fright even before a small, friendly gathering; and some others who compulsively imagine an accident while riding a vehicle. Indeed, such silly reasons to contract fear are not wanting! If we entertain such fears, our whole life is doomed to prove a horrible hell. So we must strive by all means to steer clear of such fears, and try to lead a life of boldness and bravery. In this effort, following are some hints on overcoming fear.

1. A strong body is a great help in facing fear complexes. So first and foremost, strengthen your body through regular and methodical exercises. Remember the saying: A sound mind in a sound body.

2. Strengthen your mind by reading energizing ideas and try steadily to assimilate them. How to do that? Think of those ideas again and again; apply them in your daily life. But this is possible only by keeping close company with those who have molded their lives on these ideas.

3. Discover some elders, or possibly even some among your friends, who are wise and brave. Associate with them. This will help you understand your own mental condition, and thereby root out your imaginary fears.

4. Develop moral conduct, dutifulness and a disciplined way of life, and your mind will forever be free from fear. Know for sure that moral force is the strongest force in the world!

5. Stop brooding over your little shortcomings and weaknesses. Rather strive constantly to overcome them. Solicit elder's guidance and assistance from your friends, which will be valuable.

6. Never try to draw others' sympathy by revealing to them your inabilities and weaknesses. It will only pave the way for others to misuse you and make you all the more helpless. If at all you feel the urge to open up to someone, make sure that the person is a true well-wisher of yours.

7. Even when you have fear, try to avoid giving it an expression. This will surely help you to overcome it gradually.

8. Use your will power to knock out any fearful thought the moment it raises its head; vehemently assert to yourself: I am bold. No, I am not at all afraid! I am bold! By saying this you will develop infinite self-confidence.

9. Never sit idle. Always be engaged in some constructive and creative activity. At least have some healthy recreation. And remember this wise saying: Fear is the result of too much mental activity and too little physical activity.

10. Whenever unexpected, unhappy news comes, people

tend to lose their nerve immediately. Try to overcome this tendency. Do not take it too seriously. Take it easy. After some time you will yourself feel that there was actually no need to panic. If you can keep your cool, you can more easily decide on your next move.

11. It is not a good practice to keep comparing yourself with others. Sometimes this leads to an inferiority complex, and fear creeps in. So, just be yourself. Know that you are not any less great.

12. Know this for certain: The God to whom you pray is omnipotent and all merciful. He is ever eager to come to your help. But it is necessary that you have to call upon Him, that is, you should pray to Him earnestly. Though He remains unseen, He protects his devoted children in His own inscrutable way. Only, you should not stop Him from protecting you, by doubting His unfailing presence. Hence have tremendous faith in Him.

Questions for Self-Reflection:
1. In what ways is fear protective? When does fear become harmful?

2. How do discipline, self-effort, truthfulness, and other virtues help protect us from fear?

3. What is the role of faith in reducing fear?

Coming up Next:

In the next article titled 'On the Anger Habit' the author talks about how we can use simple techniques to manage anger and redirect our energies in a positive way.

Self-Condemnation

"If I do something wrong and nobody comes to know about it, then how can I lose anything?" asked the disciple, who was obsessed by right and wrong.

The Master replied, "But you still know."

"How does that affect me?"

"Even if no one other than you knows about it, you harm yourself."

– Amul Bahl

Just Not Stories

54

12.

On the Anger Habit

Peace Pilgrim

Tremendous energy comes with anger. It's sometimes called the anger energy. Do not suppress it: that would hurt you inside. Do not express it: this would not only hurt you inside, it would cause ripples in your surroundings. What you do is transform it. You somehow use that tremendous energy constructively on a task that needs to be done, or in a beneficial form of exercise.

The best way to talk to you about this is to tell you what some people actually did. For instance, one woman washed all the windows in the house, another woman vacuumed the house whether it needed it or not, and another baked bread – nice, whole grain bread. And another one sat down and played the piano: wild marches at first, then she'd cool down and play gentle things like hymns and lullabies, and then I knew she was all right. There was a man who got out his manual lawnmower. Remember the manual lawnmower has no motor. You may never have seen one! And he mowed his big lawn. I was staying next door to him. Then one day he came over and borrowed his neighbor's power lawnmower. I spoke to him about it and he said, "Oh, without the anger energy I could never mow that big lawn with a manual lawnmower." You see, it's really tremendous energy.

Then there was this man who saved his marriage. He had such a bad temper that his young wife was about to leave him and take their two small children along. And he said, "I'm going to do something about this!" And he did. Whenever he felt a temper tantrum coming on, instead of throwing things all over the house, which had been his previous custom, he got out there and jogged. Round and round the block,

> Tremendous energy comes with anger. It's sometimes called the anger energy..

until he was all out of breath and the energy was all gone – and he saved his marriage. It worked. I saw him again years later, and I asked him, "Well, are you still jogging?" "Oh, a little bit for exercise," he said, "but I haven't had a temper tantrum for years." As you use the energy constructively you lose the anger habit.

These techniques have also worked with children. I recall one ten-year old boy. I was trying to help his mother because she was having an awful time with him. He got temper tantrums and one time, when he was not having a tantrum, I asked him "Of all the things you do what takes the most energy?" And he said, "I guess running up the hill in the back of the house." And so we found a wonderful solution. Every time his mother saw the sign of a temper tantrum, she would push him out the door and say, "Go run up the hill." It worked so well that when a teacher told me she was having a similar problem with a boy about the same age, I suggested she tell him to run around the schoolhouse, and that worked too.

> You should never try to talk to someone who is angry, because that person is not rational at that time.

Now I'll tell you about another couple. They got mad at the same time, and they decided to walk around the block. One walked one way and one walked the other way, but they met at frequent intervals. And when they could meet amicably, they walked home together and discussed what had caused their angers and what could be done to remedy it in the future. This was a very wise thing to do. You should never try to talk to someone who is angry, because that person is not rational at that time.

I'll tell one more story about a young mother. She has three children under school age and she said, "When I get mad I feel like running, but I can't. I can't leave my three small children. And I usually end up taking it out on them." I said to her, "Have you ever tried running in place?" And I could just see her running in place.

She wrote to me, "Peace, it works wonderfully well. It not only gets rid of the anger energy, but it amuses the children!"

Questions for Self-Reflection:
1. What is your way of dealing with your anger?

2. How can you practice self-care in response to the feeling of getting angry?

Coming up Next:

In the next article 'The Art of Listening', Swami Chinmayananda explains how listening has become a forgotten skill and how the lack of it causes misunderstanding and poor human relations. He describes the blind spots within us that result in poor listening and provides guidance on how we can improve our listening skills.

13.

The Art of Listening

Swami Chinmayananda

We can learn a lot from every event in life. Just as the honeybee has the special instrument (proboscis) to extract the very essence in the flowers, human beings have a special faculty (power of discrimination) to maintain the quality of life by learning the art of true listening.

Listening is the channel most often used for 'learning.' It is a vital communication function; it improves our ability of understanding, self-awareness and self-application.

Effective listening is not mere 'hearing'. In fact, we all know from our own personal experiences that mere hearing or poor listening can very well result in:

- Frustration
- Indifference
- Misunderstandings
- Misleading judgments
- Embarrassment
- Poor human relations
- Many other psychological blocks and maladjustments

Yet, listening has become almost a forgotten skill. Very often we are led to believe that: speaking represents action and power, while listening connotes weakness and apathy. We find that resistance to listening tends to be the cultural norm!

Sometimes, we pay attention to what interests us, and block out larger areas of reality. Another block to listening occurs when we form an opinion about the level of what is being said. We label the information ahead of time as unimportant, too boring, too complex, or as being nothing new. Due to such internal distractions, we become biased listeners, and our minds are tuned out rather than tuned in!

Some people fake attention – just to please the speaker!

Let us have a 'listening mind' – a mind that is open, unprejudiced, objective, alert, attentive, and relaxed.

Some have the habit of interrupting when others are talking. Personal problems sometimes manage to creep into our minds – diverting our attention – while someone else is talking. Fatigue is another limiting factor in listening, as listening takes concentration and effort. It is easier to daydream and let our minds become preoccupied when our energy level is low.

Due to such internal distractions, we become biased listeners, and our minds are tuned out rather than tuned in!

A semantic barrier is very common in most of us. No two persons have exactly the same meaning for the same word or expression. We evaluate an individual's competence and motivation through our semantic filters. We make judgments about people, based on our varied beliefs, knowledge, education, upbringing, what we understand, and what we see and perceive.

In short, the blind spots are within us. The angularities or the changing moods of the mind are barriers to effective listening. The barriers are caused by:

- Faulty memories
- Shades of ego
- Tendencies and attitudes
- Beliefs
- Images of past experiences

- Prejudices of the past
- Likes and dislikes
- Expectations and anxieties for the future

Only when we become aware of our blind spots will we be able to understand and reshape our beliefs, values, and attitudes.

Therefore, it is necessary to train the mind to widen its perspective and see things in an objective way.

Let us have a 'listening mind' – a mind that is open, unprejudiced, objective, alert, attentive, and relaxed.

Let us have a 'balanced outlook' – enjoying spiritual strength, inner stability, mental beauty, and physical perfection.

Questions for Self-Reflection:
1. If we take genuine interest and empathy in what the other person is saying, will our listening get better?

2. Most of the time, we seem to be in our 'own world'. What does it take to tune into the speaker's world?

Coming up Next:

Swami Jyotirmayananda has practical examples of what to do when you are feeling depressed, immediately to come out of it. His article also gives the viewpoint of how depression can become a source of a deep-rooted understanding of who you really are, as shown to Arjuna by Lord Krishna in the Bhagavad-Gita.

14.

Keep Your Spirits High

Swami Jyotirmayananda

It is your birthright to vibrate with strength and courage, to face life like a hero, to take things in stride with a happy heart. Until you become enlightened, however, you are bound to become depressed about your problems from time to time. The idea that you can be happy and cheerful at every moment is unrealistic. The mind will always have its ups and downs. When the clouds of dejection do enter your mind, you can drive them away by adopting the following techniques:

- Practice yoga exercises whenever you feel your spirit beginning to sink. These exercises bring harmony and balance to the mind and body. Or you may want to swim or jog or go for an invigorating walk in a beautiful natural setting. Just changing the atmosphere so that you can relax often causes your depressed mood to give way to a cheerful one.

- Do not take too seriously the negative thoughts that invade your mind when you are depressed. These thoughts are baseless. When you are dejected, you tend to imagine every terrible thing possible about yourself and become steeped in self-pity. As your mind regains its strength, these thoughts will disappear.

- Always remind yourself "All things pass away." View your dejection as a passing dark cloud and learn to wait and watch with patience. This strengthens your will and makes your personality very dynamic.

- Understand that adversity is a great teacher with a divine purpose. If you face adversity with the right attitude, it helps you to overhaul your personality by bringing the things that are hidden in your unconscious to the surface. When you are strong enough, nature has a mysterious way of presenting you with the challenging situations that are needed for your evolution. Through each difficult situation, nature is as if whispering, "Can I tell you a secret? It's going to be a little painful, but you need to hear it!"

- When nature brings you these challenging eye-openers, do not be ungrateful. Do not let depression take over and rob you of time and energy. Rather, learn to quickly push away the dark clouds that gather in your mind by keeping busy and continuing to perform your duties. Although some tasks may require a cheerful, clear mind, there are other tasks that you can perform even when the mind is more clouded. If the demands of your life in school, at work or at home do not allow you to alter your activity according to your moods, do not become upset. With patience and perseverance, you can gradually train yourself to fulfill all your responsibilities even in the most distressing of situations. If you are a student and you have a term paper due, you cannot allow yourself to linger in dejection and say, "Until this mood goes, I cannot write. I am not inspired." Rather, train yourself well and you will eventually be able to turn in your assignments on time – no matter what!

> *Just changing the atmosphere so that you can relax often causes your depressed mood to give way to a cheerful one.*

- Learn the art of promoting a positive mind by performing good actions. If you want to be happy, do not cause unhappiness in others. Having consideration for others and serving them with a generous heart will bring you joy and contentment and help you to be unaffected by the adversities of life.

- When everything seems wonderful and all your expectations are being fulfilled, don't let your mind get carried away by the feeling of elation. If you rejoice too much during prosperity, you are bound to become disappointed when the tide turns towards adversity.

- Above all, do not consider depression as a terrible problem and thus start becoming depressed about depression! Sometimes you must accept the fact that you are slightly lower in spirit. When an athlete has to jump a great height, he lowers his knees in preparation for the jump. Lowering is not always bad. Your depression is a temporary lowering of the spirit so that you can eventually jump a higher distance in spiritual understanding.

Follow the example of great men and women, and do not allow yourself to become depressed over trifles. Rather, if you must be depressed, be depressed about the fact that you are still unenlightened, that you have not yet discovered the blissful presence of God within your heart.

If depression is due to the soul's longing to understand the profound secrets of life, and because of it you seek the answers that can lead you to the highest goals, then that depression is a great blessing in disguise. This is exemplified by Arjuna's dejection in the first chapter of the *Bhagavad-Gita*. When Lord Krishna sees Arjuna's state, He is delighted

> *Learn the art of promoting a positive mind by performing good actions.*

because He knows that his disciple is now ready to receive the highest teachings. When your depression is based upon a deep urge to confront your illusions, like Arjuna, you become a true aspirant on the spiritual path and gradually discover immense spiritual strength.

> When an athlete has to jump a great height, he lowers his knees in preparation for the jump.

Once you develop a deep-rooted understanding that you are the immortal Divine Self, the embodiment of bliss, you realize how ridiculous it is to enter into a state of dejection even for a moment. It is your birthright to vibrate with strength and courage. Nothing is impossible for you. The Spirit that rules the earth and the heavens is the indweller of your heart!

Questions for Self-Reflection:
1. Can you reflect on at least three things that you can do immediately to drive away the negative thoughts affecting you at any given moment?

2. How can adversity be a teacher in one's life?

3. Can the statement 'All things will pass away' be applied in your everyday life at all times?

Coming up Next:

Have you ever wondered why you were born into your family? Is there a divine reason? Read the next article by Swami Jyotirmayananda on what is the purpose behind character building through value education at home.

Brahmacharya

The main duties of a student, whatever social order he may belong to, are for the formation of character and receiving religious as well as secular education. In Vedic times, respect and service to the teacher and contact with his exemplary life were the effective means to develop the student's moral nature. Moral and spiritual virtues do not grow without inspiration.

– Swami Shantananda

PART THREE

Relationship with Family and Friends

"What is the disease that affects all people, irrespective of age, sex, caste, creed?" asked the Master one day. "There is no such universal malady," replied the disciples. The disciples thought a little while longer, but could not come up with an answer. The Master finally said, "The universal-thinking malady is 'I can change others'. It is the biggest delusion to affect mankind."

– Amul Bahl

Just Not Stories

Often when we talk about a relationship, we seem to limit our thinking to a most restricted group, that is, a man and woman in a premarital (dating) or married state. We seem to ignore the myriad of other possible relationships in our lives equally dynamic and vital, such as, mother-father, son-daughter, cousins-uncles, and others. We assume that these relationships are different, and therefore, require other skills and qualities than what we need for successful primary relationships.

The qualities necessary for growth in any relationships are the same for all, different only in degree, not kind. In our survey, communication was mentioned as the greatest enhancer of secondary relationships. Following this were: Honesty, acceptance, forgiveness, concern, consideration, understanding, affection, respect, sharing, and a sense of humor.

– Leo F. Buscaglia

Loving Each Other

15.

Philosophical Insight into Family

Swami Jyotirmayananda

It may seem that you just came to your parents from nowhere. But if you study the law of karma and reincarnation, you learn that you are an incarnating soul – not an individual body – and you come into a family on the basis of your previous karma (actions). Further, in the process of reincarnation, you have had hundreds and hundreds of families. Although in Western society these ideas are not generally understood, in the Hindu tradition they are ingrained from childhood.

After death the spirit, according to its karma, chooses a family. You are actually the one who chooses the family to which you come. A little exercise of intellect is needed to understand that point.

If you had a strong musical inclination in your previous birth, you will now choose a family in which parents encourage you in music from childhood. Suppose in your previous birth you were inclined to worship, mysticism, meditation, yoga exercises, or other aspects of yoga sadhana (spiritual discipline), in this birth, you would be drawn into a family that would encourage you in this direction, where you would see your parents performing worship and practicing meditation.

Therefore, it is important to understand that you are

drawn to a family for a divine reason. Similarly, your parents have come in contact with you because of their karma. Their souls also need certain experiences from you. So when parents and children come together, it is not by accident.

The family is meant to help you attain God-realization. As an incarnating soul you have been a traveler who has come and gone through so many families. It is hard to believe how many thousands of fathers and mothers you have had! It is

> *You are actually the one who chooses the family to which you come.*

equally as hard to believe how many thousands of times you have been a parent, and how many thousands of children you have had! This process of reincarnation will continue until you attain God-realization.

Knowing this, you should not develop a sense of dissatisfaction: If I had been born in a different family, everything I wanted would have been given to me. I would have had wonderful toys. I would have had a wonderful car. I would have had lots of freedom. But alas, I have not been born into such a perfect family. Ideas like that should not enter your mind. You should not find fault with the family into which you belong, because that has been well arranged by a divine plan to suit all the needs of your evolution.

Real Education Begins at Home

It is not just what you learn from schools which makes you educated. The greatest teachings are given in the family – not anywhere else. In schools and colleges you may get the most advanced technical instruction, but only from the family do you learn how to develop real character and integrity.

You may get the highest grades in school. You may be offered scholarships and receive numerous awards for excellent achievement. But if you do not know how to be in harmony with your parents, your brothers and sisters, or with your husband or wife, then you have learned very little. If you do not know the art of pleasing the people around you, then you have not received the real education that allows you to be more noble and integrated and to live a truly purposeful life. In an ideal family, 'ideal' does not imply that everybody in the family is a saint. What it implies is that an ideal of harmony is followed with great sincerity of purpose. Father and mother must strive to live in harmony with each other. Children must learn to be sympathetic to the problems of their parents, and parents to be sympathetic to the problems of the children. The older members of the family must be revered, and their wisdom must serve as a guiding light to the younger people. When people live together in such an ideal family, there is great joy.

> *The more you allow yourself to be disciplined, the better and more joyous your life will be as time goes on.*

This does not mean that there will always be good times for everyone in the family. Difficult times will come every now and then, but when you share adversity with the other members of your family, everyone receives healthy encouragement and learns how to move forward with greater wisdom and strength.

The Value of Family Discipline

When you are small, you might resent your parents for disciplining you. As you grow up, however, you appreciate them because of it. As you mature you understand that it was their responsibility to raise you well. You came into their lives as a tender stranger, and it was the duty of your parents to give you a sense of values, to train you, to educate you, to prepare you for bigger responsibilities in society and for higher purposes in life.

In the Hindu culture, the first stage in life is called Brahmacharya Ashrama, the disciplinary level. The more you allow yourself to be disciplined, the better and more joyous your life will be as time goes on. But if you are not disciplined from the early stages of your life, your future will be in turmoil. That discipline implies many things: discipline of the senses, of the mind, of the intellect, and of the body.

Questions for Self-Reflection:
1. How can family be the one to help me attain God-realization? How does it contribute to my evolution?

2. What education and guidance did I receive at home that have instilled in me the sense of responsibility to be a contributing human being?

3. Are there areas in my life where I could work on developing more discipline?

Coming up Next:

In the article 'Love and Intimacy', author Dean Ornish talks about the importance of having an open heart to lead a joyful life in all relationships, not just romantic ones.

16.

Love and Intimacy

Dean Ornish

*[Dr. Ornish has directed clinical research demonstrating –
for the first time – that comprehensive lifestyle changes may
begin to reverse even severe coronary heart disease, without
drugs or surgery.]*

In my first study, many years ago, many of the men and
women talked during the group support sessions about
how the lack of love and intimacy in their relationships
in the past may have contributed to their disease. I began
to realize: Hey, that could be me in a few years if I don't
make some changes in more than just diet and meditation
and exercise. It's not enough to intellectually understand
or to write about these issues; I need to live them or I
might die. Love and survival. How extraordinary that the
people who were coming to me for healing were helping
me heal myself.

What had seemed liberating – going out with different
people – became increasingly frustrating. I knew that
I needed to make some significant changes. The same
drive that was causing these problems was not getting
my attention to begin addressing them. I wanted more
intimacy in my life.

I began to realize that an important part of my healing
was that I needed to learn to be alone. If I wanted intimacy

and love, then I first needed to learn to coexist with this pain without trying to numb it or run from it or distract myself from it in the ways that had been most familiar to me.

I spent increasing amounts of time by myself. The hardest times were when I would travel somewhere to attend a meeting or to give a lecture; afterward, I would end up in a hotel room, alone. Unlike before, I tried not to call anyone, spend time with anyone, or even watch television or read a book in order to stay with whatever feelings arose. I discovered that when I was alone, I felt as if I were disappearing.

> *Often we don't see people for who they really are. We imagine an idealized image of them and fall in love with that, projecting that image onto the other person.*

In one sense, I was. I was experiencing my self – more precisely, my 'lack' of self – without distractions or modulation. That frightening realization helped me to begin constructing a real sense of self and self-worth.

Although it was very painful, it was healing. This same pain that I had been avoiding began cutting through some of the layers and walls that had protected my heart, yet had also isolated it for so many years. I began to realize that I didn't need to be with people in order to feel I existed. Slowly, little by little, my heart began to open.

While it was important for me to define a separate self as part of my own growth, it was equally important for me to go beyond separation. So much of psychotherapy tends to focus on the first half – helping people develop an autonomous, independent, separate self – at the expense of learning how to be in an intimate, sharing relationship and finding community. I am finding that real freedom comes from choosing 'interdependence', rather than making the false choice between codependence and independence.

An Open Heart

I learned that the capacity for love and intimacy – an open heart – is so important to having a joyful life as well as to survival, in all relationships, not just romantic ones. In the past, being involved with women, whose capacity for intimacy at that time was as limited as my own, felt safe. At least I wouldn't be controlled and consumed, even if it was frustrating because the relationship wasn't very close. As my capability for intimacy grew as a result of working on these issues, I was able to make different choices. As I began to heal, I found myself in a committed relationship with a wonderful person.

I am 'not' saying that the key to happiness is finding the right Cinderella or Prince Charming, getting married, and living happily ever after. Until I had done enough work on my own obstacles to intimacy, I was incapable of being in an intimate relationship with anyone, no matter who the person was. It was not about 'finding' the right person; it was about 'being' the right person. I knew my beloved for a long time before we got into a relationship, but I couldn't even see her fully at that time.

Often we don't see people for who they really are. We imagine an idealized image of them and fall in love with that, projecting that image onto the other person. As we get to know them better, we become 'disillusioned' – quite literally, that they did not live up to our illusion of who we wanted them to be. When I was younger, I 'thought' I was in intimate relationships only because I didn't know what intimacy really meant: seeing and feeling and hearing and processing the inner world of another person instead of just projecting onto her images of who I thought she was and who I wanted her to be.

When my sweetheart and I made a commitment to the process of taking responsibility for our own behavior, rather than projecting idealized images upon each other, then the possibility of real intimacy was greatly enhanced. I began to see and to love how exquisite she really is.

This relationship is transforming my life in ways that are amazing to me. It feels like grace. Through it, I have learned how to experience happiness on a different level. Not all the time, of course, but with much greater continuity and depth

Until I had done enough work on my own obstacles to intimacy, I was incapable of being in an intimate relationship with anyone, no matter who the person was. It was not about finding the right person; it was about being the right person.

than before. The more whole I feel within myself, the greater the capacity I have for intimacy with someone else.

The great scientist Louis Pasteur once wrote, "Chance favors the prepared mind." I believe that grace favors an open heart. More precisely, grace is an open heart.

When you 'fall in love', it is usually with your illusion, your projection; it is not the same as opening your heart to your beloved. To paraphrase the author Henry Miller, I don't think I can fall in love again, so now maybe I can really learn to love someone. This idea is beautifully expressed in Psalm 1 of the book of Psalms, translated by Stephen Mitchell:

> Blessed are the man and the woman who have grown beyond their greed and have put an end to their hatred and no longer nourish illusions. But they delight in the way things are and keep their hearts open, day and night. They are like trees planted near flowing rivers, which bear fruit when they are ready. Their leaves will not fall or wither. Everything they do will succeed.

When two people commit themselves to each other, magic can begin to happen. Instead of repeating the same superficial experience with different people, I am having different, extraordinary experiences with the same person.

More than a hundred years ago, Ramakrishna talked about the importance of making a commitment to one spiritual teacher or tradition and following that path rather than going from one teacher to another. You can dig one deep well and reach a wellspring of water, or you can drill a hundred shallow, dry ones. The same is true in other relationships.

> *The more whole I feel within myself, the greater the capacity I have for intimacy with someone else.*

I had realized long before that great sex is no substitute for an open heart. What I began learning is that an open heart can lead to the most joyful and ecstatic sex. Every day, my beloved and I are learning to trust each other a little more so the walls around our hearts begin opening a little further. All the clichés come to mind – our hearts opening wider and wider, like layers of an onion being peeled away. I realize how wonderful it feels to be truly relaxed and comfortable with another person.

Guitarist Tuck Andress and singer Patti Cathcart are extraordinary musicians whose music is both powerful and loving. They are also married to each other. I once heard Tuck describing their relationship.

> My life's work is to subsume my ego into this greater whole, both musically and in our personal relationship. I spent so many years becoming a great guitar technician, practicing alone. It was a real change for me to play with someone else, learning how to listen, how to hear through her ears. I've spent time just learning how to play one note, over and

over. We've played some songs thousands of times, but there's always something fresh and new to find there. Just like our relationship. If it becomes stale, then I dig more deeply into the rut, I don't abandon it. To find the freshness that's there. The universe is right here, not over there. To leave room and space for the magic. There is the same level of detail at any level of magnification, from the subatomic to the universal, if you look closely enough.

Commitment in relationship can lead to real freedom and joy.

Questions for Self-Reflection:
1. Do you spend time being alone? For how long are you comfortable with yourself?

2. What does being comfortable with yourself mean to you?

3. How do you deal with differences with another to have a compatible loving and intimate relationship?

Coming up Next:

In the article 'Forgiving Others', authors Swami Rama and Swami Ajaya discuss the meaning of real forgiveness as an inner attitude versus an outward expression. They explain through real examples how when one practices forgiveness and love, one finds that others begin to treat you differently. The article also gives tips on dealing with people who walk all over you and strategies to be firm and forgiving of them.

17.

Forgiving Others

Swami Rama and Swami Ajaya

'I forgive you.' These three words are so powerful that they can suddenly change the darkness that we experience about us into the pure light of a new day. As soon as you experience forgiveness your whole demeanor, your attitude, and your personality change dramatically. Instead of being tormented by the hate and vengeful feelings that are carried inside in seeking justice, you experience a warm expansiveness. As you let go of those negative feelings, and of the rationalizations that gave you the excuse to get even, you find yourself beginning to experience a common bond you share with others. The sense of rigidity and of being shut off within yourself is replaced by a feeling of comfort. All this is achieved by simply saying, 'It's no big thing. I don't have to get even. I'll just let go.'

When you practice forgiveness and love, you find that others begin to treat you differently. Instead of reacting to your revengeful attitude with their own closed-off distrust, other people begin to open up and share their warmth with you. As they become aware of your forgiving attitude, they realize that they no longer have to fear your judgment and wrath. They can be themselves and be comfortable with you. Others will appreciate this to such a degree that they will open themselves to you and give whatever they can.

So, in forgiving others, we become the recipients of

comfort, peace, and happiness. It turns out that the way we treat others creates a situation that leads us to be treated in the same way.

When we forgive others we soon find that they begin to hold less against us. We need not be so fearful of their harsh judgments. This law of human existence was clearly expressed long ago in the Lord's Prayer: Forgive us our trespasses as we forgive those who trespass against us. Many people look at this statement as merely a request, asking the Lord, who is seen as separate from them, that they be forgiven the way they forgive others. But no request need be made, for there is an exact and inevitable correspondence: To the extent that we forgive others we are forgiven, and the very act of forgiving is in itself a forgiveness of ourselves. This is the law of forgiveness.

> *In forgiving others, we become the recipients of comfort, peace, and happiness. It turns out that the way we treat others creates a situation that leads us to be treated in the same way.*

There is an exact correspondence between our experience of forgiving and the experience of being forgiven. We can only open ourselves up to the experience of the others' forgiveness to the extent that we ourselves have developed a forgiving attitude. For we are being forgiven always but we do not know it when we are preoccupied with judging ourselves and others.

Practicing Forgiveness

It is not necessary to take our word that such a law exists. You can test it for yourself. Merely become aware of where and when you feel judgmental and critical of others, or whenever you feel that you have been abused and wish to get back. Then just sit quietly and think for some minutes of forgiveness until you genuinely feel yourself forgiving the other, letting go of your judgment or criticism. See for yourself how your attitude changes and what psychological effect is produced. Have you lost something or have you gained? Become aware when a critical, condemning attitude arises within you and each time work with yourself in this way. Try it for only a week and notice the reactions of others. See how relationships change.

> *The person who allows others to take advantage of him is not practicing forgiveness but is actually attempting to repress his hostile and aggressive feelings, hiding them beneath external acquiescence and acceptance.*

You might say, "How can I forgive people who have abused and mistreated me?" But if we could see more deeply into our relationships we would realize that we bring these experiences on through our own actions, we would see that there is nobody to be forgiven. The people who mistreat us are often acting out the part that we assign to them.

There is a line in a prayer by St. Francis, "It is in pardoning that we are pardoned." In the act of pardoning, we think we are doing something wonderful for the person we are forgiving, but actually we are doing something much more wonderful for ourselves. For that very act creates for us an entirely different frame of reference. Because love and forgiveness allow us to experience the world in such a harmonious way, it turns out that we are really pardoning ourselves. We are throwing off all the hate and the vengeance that we ordinarily harbor, and acquiring a new sense of inner freedom. What could be more perfect justice than that?

Some people might feel that in forgiving others they are opening themselves to being taken advantage of. They might say, "If I keep forgiving everyone they'll get away with all kinds of things." This is a misconception. In fact condemnation often does not prevent behavior but fans the flames so that the unwanted behavior increases. If the other person sees that it gets you upset, he may do the same thing again for that very reason.

Forgiving does not mean allowing people to walk all over you and abuse you. Nor does it mean that you should not try to prevent others from overstepping their bounds, from being callous and inconsiderate. Setting limits for another person is often helpful to him, whereas letting that person take advantage of you merely teaches him that he can hurt and injure others

> *Real forgiveness involves releasing all condemnation and genuinely valuing the other person.*

without concern. This does not give him a chance to develop respect and care for the other. The person who allows others to take advantage of him is not practicing forgiveness but is actually attempting to repress his hostile and aggressive feelings, hiding them beneath external acquiescence and acceptance. Often we see this quality amongst those who have been following a set of religious precepts. In trying to practice forgiveness they mistakenly decide that they should allow themselves to be used by others. While they outwardly appear to be pleasant and forgiving, there may be smoldering resentment beneath the surface. There is a vast difference between outward acquiescence, which masks resentment and a genuine inner sense of forgiveness.

Let us now look at a typical example of what happens when we confuse the outward appearance of forgiveness with the real thing: A person you have known for some time comes to visit your home and behaves rudely with you. From time to time he tells you about faults he sees in you. He takes food from the refrigerator and when he is finished eating leaves the containers out on the counter along with the dirty dishes. He stays up late at night with the TV playing loudly while you try to sleep. While you resent your guest's behavior and wish he would leave, you do not say anything to him. You have created an image in which you believe yourself to be a good, kind, and considerate person, someone who would not hurt anyone's feelings. So you keep your resentment inside secretly thinking of things that might happen to him that would 'teach him a lesson' or would even the score for the way he abused you. But outwardly you remain pleasant and cordial, cleaning up the mess he has made and sleeping with a pillow over your head.

> You may think that you are practicing forgiveness, but your outward behavior does not reflect your true feelings.

You may think that you are practicing forgiveness, but your outward behavior does not reflect your true feelings. While you pretend that you are acting in a forgiving manner, a closer examination may actually reveal subtle critical remarks and hostile thoughts. This situation may lead to any number of consequences. For example, you may develop physical symptoms as a result of the pressure of unreleased emotions. Or perhaps you will continue to collect a list of all the things your visitor has done wrong until you feel 'righteous and justified' in telling him how he has abused you. Then you feel the walled-in anger filling you and bursting out in a tirade as you tell him of all the inconsiderate acts he has committed. It feels good to be releasing these feelings at last.

In this characterization forgiveness was understood as an attitude, which expressed itself in outward acquiescence. But actually forgiveness is an inner attitude, which is not necessarily revealed by outwardly giving in to someone. All too often in many areas of our lives we try to cheat ourselves, and others by substituting an outer appearance for the real thing. We mimic genuine forgiveness until sooner or later our true sentiments are revealed beneath the façade. Real forgiveness involves releasing all condemnation and genuinely valuing the other person. Outwardly you may still find it necessary to be firm and to set clear limits on another. But this firmness can be expressed from an inner and interpersonal harmony rather than a sense of justified annoyance or criticism.

Questions for Self-Reflection:
1. Do you forgive easily? Is it an outward appearance of forgiveness or an inner attitude?

2. If a person's detestable or abusive behavior is not directed at you, would you openly confront him/her to let them know it is not acceptable? Why or why not?

3. How does one balance the act of true forgiveness and standing up against being taken advantage of?

Coming up Next:

Often times we deal with people who are not spiritually inclined and relating to them can cause conflicts for many reasons. Author Vinita Hampton Wright looks at Five Ways to Relate to Family Members Spiritually with practical tips on how to engage people to have more fulfilling relationships.

Forgiveness

*Don't just ask for forgiveness: forgive yourself.
The Lord cannot forgive you as long as you are
feeling guilty and bringing up the same idea
again and again in your mind. If you accept and
acknowledge the mistake, it is forgiven. Have faith
in this assertion of our scriptures.*

– Swami Chinmayananda

18.

Five Ways to Relate to Family Members Spiritually

Vinita Hampton Wright

It can be quite difficult to express personal spirituality in family situations that are not particularly friendly toward religion. Especially if a family has experienced religion as judgmental or strident – and all it takes is one or two people to create that atmosphere – the door to spiritual conversations and expressions might be shut tightly.

But if we loosen up on our concept of spirituality, we might discover that we can relate quite spiritually with people who otherwise would resist religion.

1. Extend your gratitude practices to the people you love.

I believe more and more – and I think I'm with St. Ignatius Loyola on this – that gratitude is foundational to spiritual health. If I go through life in a posture of gratitude, that will transform so many situations that would otherwise deteriorate. What I need to remember is that gratitude toward God is key – but gratitude toward others is important too. If I make a practice of expressing to others, on a regular basis, what I'm grateful for in terms of their personality, gifts, efforts, and so on, I will be relating to people in a spiritually healthy way. And that will make a good impact sooner or later. I may help someone recognize her gifts, or I may help another be kinder to himself.

2. Help others become comfortable with silence.

People who can become comfortable when there's no noise, activity, or talking will be better equipped to handle stress, problems, questions, and all sorts of emotions. I can help others make friends with silence by being silent with them, by showing them that I'm fine with sitting together for a while without saying anything, and by not rushing to get an answer or to form an opinion. I can model this sort of calm, and eventually others who spend time with me might just come to value that spiritual discipline as well.

3. Receive – always – a person as he or she is.

It can be especially difficult to withhold judgment with members of your own family or circle of friends, because we feel responsible for those we love. But if we can relax, trust God, and simply receive loved ones in whatever shape they're in, they will be more likely to open up to us – maybe not right now, maybe some time from now – and allow us to be part of the conversation about the struggling marriage or the drug problem or the

> What I need to remember is that gratitude toward God is key – but gratitude toward others is important too.

personality flaws that are making it difficult to hold down a job. Meeting a person first with judgment will send that person far away, even if she lives in the same house. And many people have been conditioned to think that if they turn to religion the first thing they will experience is God's horrible judgment and anger. We have to model God's open arms and forgiveness; otherwise how will anyone know the truth about Divine Love?

4. Reject cynicism and promote hope.

It can be a real challenge to reign in the negativity when people get together. If you have a certain friend or relative who has honed criticism and sarcasm to fine points, then pray for the patience to be just as energetic with encouragement and praise. When the conversation comes to a dark, thudding halt because everyone has helped everyone else become even more depressed about world affairs, dare to tell the story of someone doing a wonderful, brave thing. Of course you can't always be on task with this, or it can seem that you're arguing just as much as the other person, only with a positive emphasis. But hope is a spiritual practice, and sometimes we have to counter despair quite purposefully.

> Meeting a person first with judgment will send that person far away, even if she lives in the same house.

5. Care more about healing than about justice.

I am doing my best to swear off vengeance, because the world is rank with it, and we have to make a stand. I even refrain from seeing some films because it's clear that vengeance is the major theme. I become vengeful easily enough on my own – I don't need cultural reinforcement. So when dealing with daily issues, even conversations at a family gathering, I hope to not chime in about people getting what they deserve. And if a friend or family member is the one who's receiving the harsh judgment, I may be the only voice advocating not for vengeance and punishment but for mercy and growth.

Well, these are just ideas. What do you think?

Questions for Self-Reflection:
1. Do you know people who are hard to relate to in a spiritual way? How do you deal with them?

2.Can you think of other ways that would lead to spiritual engagements with family and friends?

Coming up Next:

In the article 'The Ten Commandments of Marriage', author J.P Vaswani explains in the simplest and most practical way on how to keep your love fresh during your marriage and have a healthy and happy life together with your spouse.

Cherish your human connections - your relationships with friends and family.
– Barbara Bush

19.

The Ten Commandments of Marriage

J. P. Vaswani

Let me pass on to you ten practical suggestions. I sometimes refer to them as the ten commandments of marriage.

1. The very first commandment is – 'avoid the next quarrel'. If one of you is in a mood to quarrel, the other one should be patient. His or her turn will come at the right time. But both should not lose their temper at the same time.

2. The second commandment of marriage is – 'be a good listener'. Listen to what the other person has to say. We like to talk but are not prepared to listen. Let us be good listeners. Of a couple it was said – in the days of courtship he talked and she listened. On their honeymoon, she talked and he listened. Now that they are settled down in their own home, both talk and the neighbors listen!

3. The third commandment of marriage is – appreciate your spouse. Everyone loves to be appreciated. Do not find fault with your spouse when you are in the midst of other people. Leonardo da Vinci said, "Reprove your friend in secret, praise him before others." When we appreciate others, we help to draw out the best in them.

4. The fourth commandment is – keep your love fresh!

After marriage, spouses take each other for granted. Women have complained to me, "There was a time when our husbands gave us many promises, made many vows, took great interest in what we did. All this has become a part of history. Now they take us for granted". Therefore, keep your love fresh.

5. The fifth commandment is – do not expect perfection of each other. No man or woman is ever perfect. It was Jesus who said, "Call me not perfect. Only the Father in heaven is perfect!" Marriage involves two imperfect human beings joining together. Accept your spouse for what he or she is, not for what he or she would be, could be or should be.

6. The sixth commandment is – be a good 'forgiver'. To make marriage a success, to make it a source of happiness and harmony, you have to forgive much. It is the prerogative of marriage to give and give and give and forgive – and never be tired of giving and forgiving. "How many times shall I forgive?" asked a husband. "Shall I forgive seven times," "No," came the answer, "You must forgive seventy times seven." Seventy times seven is 490 times which means you must forgive without counting. And a wife complained, "I have been forgiving until I can forgive no longer. I have forgiven and received nothing in return." And she was told, "Continue to forgive without expecting anything in return."

7. The seventh commandment of marriage is – you must be patient, loving, understanding, kind and true to each other.

8. The eighth commandment is – develop a healthy sense of humor. If two people have to live with each other, they must develop a healthy sense of humor. They must learn to laugh and make the other laugh.

9. The ninth commandment is – if ever there is a

misunderstanding; do not hide your feelings. Do not hesitate to discuss whatever is in your hearts, freely and without fear.

10. The tenth and the most important commandment is – everyday, you must find time to sit together and praise the Lord and thank Him for having brought the two of you together.

Questions for Self-Reflection:

1. It may be necessary to sacrifice what one likes to do for the sake of harmony in the marriage. How can you bring clarity in your understanding that being happy together is more important than being happy for just yourself?

2. When you want to discuss your feelings during a misunderstanding, do you always make sure that you are in state of calm, not one of anger?

Coming up Next:

Using the theories of Alfred Adler, Ichiro Kishimi and Fumitake Koga explore the relationship between the individual and the world and why one is not the center of the world but part of a community.

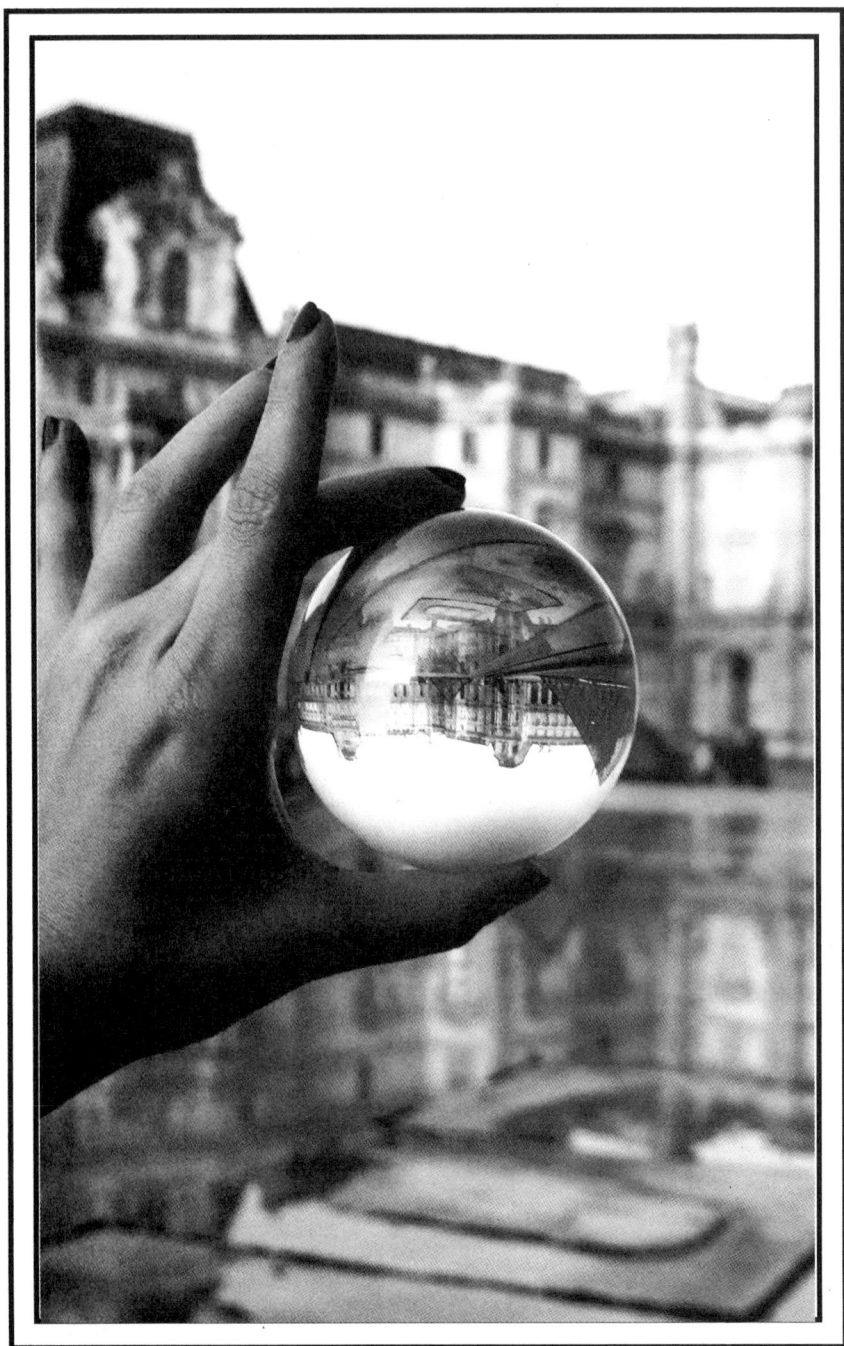

PART FOUR

Relationship with the World

In God's creation one can see variety. Even though we see
differences there is one thing that is common in all of us and
that is the presence of the God Principle.

Swami Shantananda

The Hindus call their religion 'The Eternal Dharma'-Sanatana Dharma. The word dharma comes from the Sanskrit root dhr, which means 'to hold' or 'to support'. Therefore, dharma stands for that which holds up or supports the existence of a thing. Everything in the whole universe has its own dharma because it must rely on something for its existence. It is the essential nature of a thing without which it cannot exist. The essential nature of a thing is, therefore, called its dharma. For example, fire burns; its power of burning is its dharma. A human being also has an essential nature that upholds his existence as distinct from the rest of creation. That essential nature must be his dharma. So naturally we ask: "What is this essential nature, or dharma, of a human being?"

The Hindus emphatically uphold that the dharma of a human being is his capacity to become divine, which distinguishes him from all other beings. Some may ask: "How can a human being become divine?" The equally startling reply is: "Because divinity is already in us!" This truth has been clearly stated in all the major scriptures of the world. All duties are considered dharma in our scriptures. Our duties toward relatives, friends, the community, nation and the world, obligations to our environment, our affections, reverence, charity and sense of goodwill are all dharma. In and through such actions – physical, mental and intellectual – man can bring forth the expression of his true dharma, which is his divine status as the all-pervading Self. To live truly as the Ätman, and to express its infinite perfection through all our actions and in all our contacts with the world, we will rediscover our true dharma.

Swami Chinmayananda

20.

You are Not at the Center of the World

Ichiro Kishimi and Fumiake Koga

PHILOSOPHER: Let's go over things in order. First of all, each of us is a member of a community, and that is where we belong. Feeling that one has one's own place of refuge within the community, feeling that 'it's okay to be here' and having a sense of belonging – these are basic human desires. Whether it is one's studies, work, or friendships, or ones love or marriage, all these things are connected to one's search for places and relationships in which one can feel 'it's okay to be here.' Wouldn't you agree?

YOUTH: Ah, yes, I do! That's it exactly!

PHILOSOPHER: And the protagonist in one's life is the 'I.' There is nothing wrong with the train of thought up to this point. But the 'I' does not rule the center of the world. While the 'I' is life's protagonist, it is never more than a member of the community and a part of the whole.

YOUTH: A part of the whole?

PHILOSOPHER: People who have concern only for themselves think that they are at the center of the world. To such people, others are merely 'people who will do something for me'. They half genuinely believe that everyone else exists to serve them and should give precedence to their feelings.

98

YOUTH: Just like a prince or a princess.

PHILOSOPHER: Yes, exactly. They make a leap from being 'life's protagonist' to becoming 'the world's protagonist'. For this reason, whenever they come into contact with another person, all they can think is, "What will this person give me?" However – and this is something that does not hold true for princes and princesses – this expectation is not going to be satisfied on every occasion. Because other people are not living to satisfy your expectations.

YOUTH: Indeed.

PHILOSOPHER: Then, when those expectations are not satisfied, they become deeply disillusioned and feel as if they have been horribly insulted. And they become resentful, and think, "That person didn't do anything for me. That person let me down. That person isn't my comrade anymore. He's my enemy." People who hold the belief that they are the center of the world always end up losing their comrades before long.

YOUTH: That's strange. Didn't you say that we are living in a subjective world: As long as the world is a subjective space, I am the only one who can be at its center. I won't let anyone else be there.

PHILOSOPHER: I think that when you speak of 'the world', what you have in mind is something like a map of the world.

YOUTH: A map of the world? What are you talking about?

PHILOSOPHER: For example, on the map of the world used in France, the Americas are located on the left side, and Asia is on the right. Europe and France are depicted at the center of the map, of course. The map of the world used in China, on the other hand, shows the Americas on the right side and Europe on the left. French people who see the Chinese map of the world will most likely experience a difficult-to-describe sense of incongruity, as if they have been driven unjustly to the fringes, or cut out of the world arbitrarily.

YOUTH: Yes, I see your point.

PHILOSOPHER: But what happens when a globe is used to represent the world? Because with a globe, you can look at the world with France at the center, or China, or Brazil, for that matter. Every place is central, and no place is, at the same time. The globe may be dotted with an infinite number of centers, in accordance with the viewer's location and angle of view. That is the nature of a globe.

YOUTH: Hmm, that is true.

PHILOSOPHER: Think of what I said earlier – that you are not the center of the world – as being the same thing. You are a part of a community, not its center.

YOUTH: I am not the center of the world. Our world is a globe, not a map that has been cut out on a plane. Well, I can understand that in theory, anyway. But why do I have to be aware of the fact that I'm not the center of the world?

PHILOSOPHER: Now we will go back to where we started. All of us are searching for the sense of belonging, that 'it's okay to be here.' In Adlerian psychology, however, a sense of belonging is something that one can attain only by making an active commitment to the community of one's own accord, and not simply by being here.

YOUTH: By making an active commitment? What does one do, exactly?

PHILOSOPHER: One faces one's life tasks. In other words, one takes steps forward on one's own, without avoiding the tasks of the interpersonal relations of work, friendship, and love.

If you are 'the center of the world, you will have no thoughts whatsoever regarding commitment to the community; because everyone else is 'someone who will do something for me', and there is no need for you to do things yourself. But you are not the center of the world, and neither am I. One has to stand on one's own two feet, and take one's own steps forward with the tasks of interpersonal relations. One needs to think not, "What will this person give me? but rather, What can I give to this person?" That is commitment to the community.

YOUTH: It is because when one gives something that one can find one's refuge?

PHILOSOPHER: That's right. A sense of belonging is something that one acquires through one's own efforts – it is not something one is endowed with at birth. Community feeling is the much debated key concept of Adlerian psychology.

Questions for Self-Reflection:
1. How often do you volunteer to contribute to the welfare of others?

2. How often do you hope that the work that you do positively influences others?

3. How often do you hope to leave the world better than you found it?

Coming up Next:

Gabriela Díaz Musmanni explores 'Four Ways that Spirituality can Revolutionize Climate Adaptation'. Climate change is the most urgent issue that concerns each and every one of us on earth. Is it an isolated and secular issue or can spiritual awareness bring a change?

21.

Four Ways That Spirituality Can Revolutionize Climate Adaptation

Gabriela Díaz Musmanni

What if the solution to the world's climate challenges didn't cost a penny, require paperwork or government approval?

According to several faith communities, it doesn't. The solution lies within every one of us and it involves a change of awareness and our relationship with nature.

"The solution becomes a question of individual, personal choice, and a decision that I am going to turn things around, in my life, 180 degrees. Simply by the change of consciousness, a change of awareness, and living in the awareness of my own spiritual identity. Because from there, then, our relationship with nature would completely change," said Valériane Bernard, Brahma Kumaris representative to the United Nations in Geneva.

In October 2021, the Global Center on Adaptation's Water Adaptation Community (WAC) and the ICOMOS International Scientific Committee on Water and Heritage (ISC Water) organized the webinar Water and Spirituality for Climate Adaptation ahead of the dialogue among spiritual leaders that will take place at the UN Mid-term Review of the Water Action Decade in New York in 2023.

Spiritual leaders from different faiths convened to

exchange insights on how spirituality can not only provide resilience to climate impacts, but help boost adaptation. The event was also held to launch WAC's Community of Practice on Water and Culture.

The spiritual leaders, who tuned in from all over the world, proved that faith communities have a lot to say about climate issues. As noted by Maria Hammershøy, the Vice-President of Justice and Peace Europe and Secretary General of Caritas Denmark, faith communities often step up to help after climate disasters strike. Their insights, sacred relationship with our natural elements and traditional practices can advance adaptation, protect nature, and are crucial, although not always present in climate discussions.

> ... *"Nature protects when she is protected"*

The following are four practices that spiritual communities promote, which can help individuals take matters into their own hands for the planet's common good.

1. Understanding the Root of the Problem

A lack of spirituality could be at the root of the global problems we face today, including the climate emergency, according to some of the leaders gathered for the WAC webinar.

"Could it be that we have forgotten the sanctity of life, overlooking what is the most important aspect of each human being, that is the inner being, the spiritual being?" asked Bernard, explaining that in today's world, consumerism and materialism have moved us away from our understanding of the spirit or 'life force.'

"Equally there is no respect for other forms of life and no sooner respect for other human beings," she added.

Iberê Guarani Mbyá, Leader of the Guaraní people of

Brazil, who walked 12 hours to find internet to participate in the webinar, expressed that our fast-paced lives shield us from spirituality and simplicity.

"We live in a country, where there are 83,000 kilometers of rivers – and all of them are polluted. 32 million Brazilians do not have running water. And 11.5 million live in homes with more than three people per room. 5.8 million do not have a bathroom," he said.

"We, the original people, respect everything that surrounds us, because everything that surrounds us is us," he said, adding "perhaps the civilized people, perhaps the ones who emerged, were born and grew up in cities do not know it, have never come to know the beauty of simplicity and imperfection. We, being simple and imperfect, learn from everything around us. A society of speed, a society incapable of experience; a society in which nothing touches the heart."

> "Water is a blessing and water is used as a blessing.

2. Realizing our Oneness

At the spirit level, we are all one and the same. In the poetic words of Guarani Mbyá, humans, animals and nature are all related:

"We are kin to all that lives and all that pulsates. We are kin to all that flows, and to all that unfolds. We are all kin. The hawk is kin to the snake that unfolds itself, as if unsheathed. The wind blowing on the water, in the air, forming words, these are the beautiful words of our grandparents. We are relatives of those who live in the water, together with Jasuka Sy Ete, the first mother, the great-great-grandmother of the grandmother we see. We are relatives of the dead and of the mountains; kin to Yamandu, whose heart is the sun, the great-great-grandfather of this sun that we see," said the Guaraní leader, who is a doctoral student of Social Anthropology from the University of Brasilia.

Dharma Master Hsin Tao, Founding Abbot of the Ling Jiou Mountain Buddhist Society and Founder of the Museum of World Religions, explained that spirituality and ecology are inseparable and that once we understand our interconnectedness with nature and others, compassion will inevitably follow, leading us to protect the Earth and all living beings.

"We are talking about the vision of adapting to climate change from the perspective of Buddhism. Buddhism is returning to the original spiritual nature, realizing that all things have the same root and the same life entity, therefore transcending the material phenomena of the world, and then we can send out compassion and great love from our inherent spirituality" he said.

3. Establishing a sacred relationship with the elements

Mona Polacca, a Native American Spiritual Elder and member of the International Council of Thirteen Indigenous Grandmothers, shared that her people, the 'People of the Blue Green Water' who live at the bottom of the Grand Canyon, have a sacred relationship with their surroundings, particularly water.

"When it comes to indigenous wisdom and knowledge, we do not have sacred texts. We do not have scholars of our spirituality, our spiritual practices and beliefs. What we base our wisdom and knowledge on is our relationship with the place where we live, the place where we come from, which we consider our life," she said.

"We are all related through the basic foundations of life, of which water is the first foundation, according to the teachings I follow. We were inside water in our mother's womb, we lived there for three quarters of a year. And when it was time for us to be born, the water came out of our mother's womb and we followed it into this world. And because of that we call the water our Sacred Mother Water," Polacca said.

4. Practical Solutions to Adapt to Climate Change

According to Dharma Master Hsin Tao, all awakening must start with education. This is why he founded the University for Life and Peace, a global education platform where he plans to promote 'Spiritual Ecology,' which he defines as 'the discovery that everything has spirituality'.

"Through the platform of university education, we will integrate spiritual ecology into various professional fields, achieving cross-cooperation, and generate actions based on spiritual awakening and knowledge. Spirituality, which is similar across religions, is like water, irrigating a multi-connected, mutually dependent and benefitting ecology, guiding us to love the earth together," he said.

Polacca, who has a Master of Social Work degree and serves on several United Nations committees on indigenous people's issues, expressed that her people have a sacred relationship with water. But, how does that translate into action and how can such a relationship be achieved?

> *Spirituality, which is similar across religions, is like water, irrigating a multi-connected, mutually dependent and benefitting ecology, guiding us to love the earth together.*

Polacca shared that indigenous practices include Water Ethics – the simple practice of honoring water.

"Water is a blessing and water is used as a blessing. In my teachings, when I come upon water, it's important for me, for my wellbeing and spiritually, mentally, emotionally, physically, to acknowledge the water in a sacred manner. To approach it with respect and humility. To introduce myself to it and acknowledge that it is my life.... In our ceremonies we have time where we take a moment to acknowledge the water.... We sprinkle the water on Mother Earth as an offering to Mother Earth and all of life on Mother Earth," she said.

Bernard spoke about the Law of Karma, stating that 'nature protects when she is protected'. In practical terms, the Brahma Kumaris perform actions such as tree planting, caring for forests, water management and purification work, and awareness raising to save water and promote vegetarianism.

"As you might be aware, a lot of the water of our Earth is used by the food industry to grow meat, which is something that produces a lot of carbon dioxide and also consumes a lot of water," she said.

For more on this topic refer to the Mananam Series book titled: Egocentric to Ecocentric.

Questions for Self-Reflection:
1. How can one's individual outlook and actions towards the environment affect climate change?

2. How does the 'Law of Karma' relate to the environment?

3. What are some doable, practical actions to influence climate change as an individual and as a community?

Coming up Next:

Read next how Mark Sorbara makes a convincing case for the most effective method of giving help – through knowledge!

Dr. Suzuki's most effective ways to help conserve nature are the result of being asked "what can I do?" by members of audiences whenever he speaks. Here, below, are those 10 things as part of the Nature Challenge.

1. Reduce home energy use by 10%

2. Choose an energy-efficient home and appliances

3. Don't use pesticides

4. Eat meat-free meals one day a week

5. Buy locally grown and produced food

6. Choose a fuel-efficient vehicle

7. Walk, bike, carpool or take transit

8. Choose a home close to work or school

9. Support alternative transportation

10. Learn more and share with others.

The Challenge is to pick at least three steps and sign up by visiting www.davidsuzuki.org and following the links. It's an easy and effective way to make a difference.

Dr. David Suzuki is an award-winning scientist, environmentalist, and broadcaster.

22.

Helping Others the Right Way

Mark Sorbara

How often do North Americans hear about Africa? And when they do, what do they hear? These simple questions are what sparked my interest in Africa. I grew up in a society whose views of Africa are dominated by the fly-faced, kwashiorkor-bellied children of the World Vision commercials. But Africa's communities, cultures, religions, and people have always, and will continue to be, more than just the poster children for war, famine, disease, and pity. Like most of the world, Africa faces many challenges that require the solidarity and support of the world community. Knowledge is the most important factor in achieving such unity. That being said, we must not allow our commitment to altruism to be skewed by a stereotyped view of the less fortunate. As simple as it may seem, time must be taken to open our minds and learn, so we can finally begin to understand that the only difference between a wealthy North American and a poor African is material. Pity is the most destructive element of selflessness, because it creates a superiority complex in the giver and an inferiority complex in the receiver. True altruism is the child of knowledge, not the other way around.

This is where my story begins. During my university days I was fortunate enough on many occasions to be able to spend time in sub-Saharan Africa and with many different people.

From studying abroad in Uganda, Zimbabwe, and Mali to a volunteer stint in Ghana, I became surrounded by many Westerners who wanted to make a difference in the lives of 'poor' Africans. In Ghana, North Americans would come with their laptops, digital cameras, and safari clothes for three to four weeks, intent on making an impact. After three weeks and almost no impact, some of the disappointed volunteers returned home, not with good stories of Ghanaians,

> ...we must not allow our commitment to altruism to be skewed by a stereotyped view of the less fortunate.

Ghanaian food, or Ghanaian clothing but stories of the 'poor,' 'uneducated,' 'hungry' Ghanaians that needed our help! Instead of taking time to learn about Ghana during their short stay and returning home as ambassadors for Ghana, those volunteers simply rejoined the ranks of the World Vision pity-peddling North Americans.

In Mali, while enjoying an orange juice in an open air café in Bamako with some fellow students, one of them asked me: "What can I do right now to make a difference; I see all this poverty and need, and I know with the little money I have I can make a difference, but how?" I told my fellow student that instead of worrying about who or where to use his money before returning home, why not spread the word about Malians, not about their 'poverty' or 'misery,' but begin the process of knowledge.

During a break between classes while I was at Makerere University in Uganda studying development with the School for International Training, a fellow Ugandan student and I were discussing Ugandan politics. On our way back to class he asked me, "Are you going to come back to Uganda and open an NGO and help in Uganda's development?" My response was simple and straightforward. I told him that I was not here to 'save' Ugandans or spread aid dollars. Rather, I was here to learn about Uganda and take the knowledge back to North America so I could teach others that Uganda is more than just a 'poverty's showroom.' Ugandans are no different than North Americans; they may be materially less endowed, but that means nothing; and respect for their similarities is the first step in addressing the world's challenges.

A few days after I had arrived in Zimbabwe, I walked to the corner store near where we were staying to purchase some postcards to mail home. I wanted to show my friends and family the gleaming glass skyscrapers of downtown Harare. I could have sent them the typical safari postcard, but I wanted to send the message that Africa, in particular Zimbabwe, is not an elephant-ridden and zebra-filled savannah. It has computers, bank machines, and office towers like in North America. Although to most people this may seem like a useless gesture, to me it was an important step in addressing the stereotypes and binary views about Africa. These views are inhibiting us from addressing global challenges. The seeds of learning must be planted before the tree of knowledge can grow and bear fruit. The seed needs fertile soil to grow, and this is where individual change plays an important role, as the inscription on a 12th century tomb illustrates:

> *Sometimes opening our minds and learning about others can be the most important altruistic act and the right way to help.*

> When I was a child I thought I could change the world. When I was a youth I thought I could change my country. When I married I thought I could change my family. Now I am dying and I realize that I can change myself and perhaps by changing myself I could change my family and then my country and finally the whole world.

Most ideas are not new, but the will to follow through with them is! Knowledge may not be the most glamorous or exciting aspect of helping, but it is the most important. If one does not attempt to learn and gain knowledge about those he or she wishes to help, the idea of cooperation disappears. In its place we find a patronizing, one-sided relationship based on pity, and ideas of 'us' and 'them' become the defining characteristics of goodwill and generosity.

Respect is the foundation of goodwill. By taking the time to learn about a person's community, religion, and culture, regardless of their material standing, we can show that we respect people for who they are, not for what they have or do not have. Giving time, money, and material items to those less fortunate may clear our conscience, but if it is not coupled with mutual respect based on knowledge, the more fortunate will never overcome the superficial material divide. Sometimes opening our minds and learning about others can be the most important altruistic act and the right way to help.

Questions for Self-Reflection:
1. Why is feeling pity for someone in need considered the most damaging attitude to help? How does it harm the giver and the receiver?

2. How does understanding someone's situation be the first step for altruism?

3. Why is knowledge the most important aspect of helping?

Coming up Next:

Read how the famous author Chitra Banerjee Divakaruni received the precious gifts on practicing balance in her life from Swami Chinmayananda himself when she was a young adult. She shares her treasured interactions with Swamiji in this heartfelt personal essay.

23.

What Swami Chinmayananda Taught Me About Balance

Chitra Banerjee Divakaruni

Much of what I know of spirituality I learned from Swami Chinmayananda, whom I had the blessed fortune to meet and get to know when I was in my twenties in California, where at that time he would visit almost every summer. That he taught me about spirituality will not surprise anyone; he was, after all, an amazing spiritual master. What might be somewhat more surprising is that he taught me many things about daily living as well. As a young person living in a country where I was constantly trying to balance both ends of the spectrum of being Indian and American, I found his lessons most helpful. Later, as a mother bringing up children in this country, I found them useful in a whole different way. I will try to share some of his gifts in this article.

One of my earliest memories of Swamiji was at Krishnalaya, in Piercy, in the mountains of Northern California, the center where he was offering a Geeta camp. During the adult classes, which I attended, he was strict and focused. But in the afternoons, in between a brief rest and important Chinmaya Mission matters on which he was constantly consulted, he would find some time to 'hang out' with the children. There was a swimming pool at Krishnalaya at the time; he would sit on the edge of the pool, feet dangling in the water, laughing and joking with the children, getting splashed as they jumped into the pool, and splashing them back. There was a wonderful playfulness about Swamiji. He knew when to be serious and when to lighten the atmosphere. He taught that to the children, too: there was time for study and effort, and time for relaxation and

> *Balance is crucial in our lives, and it doesn't matter how old we are.*

play. He often told parents not to be overly strict. Yes, children should study and do well in school, he said. But give them time to be children, to enjoy childhood and friendship. To Bala Vihar teachers he said, make learning fun. They should have fun coming to Bala Vihar every weekend. Then the values we teach will remain with them, because they will remember them with fondness. This is something I internalized for myself and tried to teach my children: life should be a balance of work and fun, strictness and laughter; it is important to set aside time for relaxation and joy.

Another thing I learned from Swamiji was to be comfortable where life had placed me and be appreciative of what – or who – was around me. He often said, "Bloom where you are planted." I loved this saying; it is one I have repeated to my own children. To parents who often bemoaned to him the fact that their children were becoming too 'westernized', Swamiji would say, "You made the decision to live in America. Now you cannot expect your children to live like you used to live in India, or to think like you used to think." He was fully aware that young people needed to feel comfortable outside the home – at school or at work, and he was quite confident that they could do that without losing their Indian values. I remember him asking the youth who their friends were. He would tell them it was good to have friends of various backgrounds, as long they had good values. He himself taught by example – many of his close followers were non-Indians, and he enjoyed spending time with them and never tired of answering their questions. I even remember him watching popular TV shows and asking questions about American customs so that he could then use them as examples in his evening lectures! Several of his early non-Indian devotees went on to be powerful supporters of the Mission, with important and responsible roles.

Balance, the middle path, the golden mean. It is what Sri Krishna teaches in Chapter 6 of the Gita, one of my favorite chapters:

> *Yoga becomes a destroyer of sorrow for one whose eating and movements are regulated, whose effort in work is moderate, and whose sleep and wakefulness are temperate.*

It is an excellent lesson for the young because the youthful years are a time (I know this from my own life and from observing my children) when we tend to extremes. We are quick to get over-excited about certain issues. We 'love' certain things and people and circumstances and we 'hate' others. Swamiji understood this tendency of the not-yet-mature mind and gently encouraged us to be balanced in our lifestyle, values, activities, habits, likes and dislikes.

Along with disciplining ourselves, we will also practice being kind to ourselves. That is an important aspect of balance.

But the most important thing that Swami Chinmayananda taught me about balance was during a treasured one-on-one conversation I had with him in Krishnalaya. I had been having problems with certain relatives who I felt were treating me wrongly. I complained bitterly to Swamiji, with tears in my eyes. Then I asked him what I should do. I was angry with these people and felt wrongfully injured; still, a part of me wanted to do the right thing.

Swamiji smiled at me with great kindness and patience, though many people before me must have brought the same problem to him. He did not scold me or tell me I was behaving immaturely, though looking back, I see that I was! He quoted chapter 6 of the Gita again, verse 9 where Krishna tells Arjuna

> *Balance, the middle path, the golden mean. It is what Sri Krishna teaches in Chapter 6 of the Gita.*

that the wise man behaves the same way towards friends and enemies. Then he said, "Practice samatva. When the mind is equanimous, nothing can trouble it." And finally, he said, "Love all who come into your life; then you will know exactly how to handle them."

This was his final lesson to me on balance, for which I am eternally grateful. It is as valuable and relevant today as it was 40 years ago, when he gifted it to me.

Balance is crucial in our lives, and it doesn't matter how old we are. My children need it and I need it, and if I ever have grandchildren, they will need it too. Balance in our 'external' lives is important, and a good place to start, especially for those of us who walk the tightrope between two very different cultures. If we are wise, we will discipline ourselves and regulate our lives so that we are well-balanced between the values of the West and the East, between work and leisure, between family and friends. Along with disciplining ourselves, we will also practice being kind to ourselves. That is an important aspect of balance.

But what is most important is inner balance, deep down. Samatvam. To balance our minds and intellects, to value and practice equanimity. If by divine blessing we gain that, and the calm understanding of ever-changing samsara that it brings, the problems in our lives will take care of themselves. We will know how to deal with the situations that arise; we will know how to treat people as they need to be treated. There will be no more enemies. There will only be love.

Questions for Self-Reflection:

1. How can we practice samatvam externally, and internally?

2. How can moderation in all aspects of life help one overcome sorrow?

3. Is it possible to love all who come into our lives?

Coming up Next:

Through self-control (Brahmacharya), non-injury (Ahimsa), and living a life with convictions (Satyam), one can reach the supreme heights in any field of life., Swami Chinmayananda explains how these three principles, when followed sincerely, integrate our personality and makes us fit for spiritual evolution.

24.

The Three Principles of Life

Swami Chinmayananda

To realize our full spiritual Nature is to experience the fullness of life. As long as we have not attained this state of being, our intellect will continue to suggest methods for overcoming feelings of imperfection, which manifest as desires. Desires are nothing but an expression of the ignorance of our real Nature. This ignorance has made us identify with the body, mind, and intellect, and is the cause of our egocentric life of pains and limitations. Therefore, there is no achievement more sacred and glorious than the realization of our true identity with the unlimited, eternal Self.

The purpose of religion is to eliminate ignorance through spiritual practices until the devotee comes to gain the light of wisdom. Ignorance, manifesting as desires on the mental plane, extend themselves as actions in the world. Therefore, spiritual masters advise that the most practical way of overcoming ignorance is through controlling our actions. They suggest that we first purify, and regulate these actions. All religions advocate qualities such as goodness, kindness, tolerance, mercy, and selflessness. They insist on moral and ethical perfection as the fundamental condition for spiritual evolution. Without these qualities we will end up far short of the goal, even after a lifetime of devotion and worship.

Let us try to understand the scope of these moral and ethical values as explained in Hinduism. The three corner stones upon which the temple of Hinduism has been built are self-control, non-injury, and truthfulness. The vast amount of spiritual literature in India is nothing but annotations, amplifications, and commentaries upon these three principles. Ancient Indians planned their individual, communal, and national life upon these three fundamental duties.

When these values are practiced they enable us to master our mind, which leads to mastery over ourselves, and the world around us. Although these principles are essentially the same in all religions, differences may appear due to the way in which they were presented to meet the needs of the people of the time. These three fundamental moral codes of behavior are: self-control (brahmacharya), non-injury (ahimsa), and truthfulness (satyam). They are the source of all values, and refer to the three layers of our personality: physical, emotional, and intellectual.

Self-Control

The physical body longs for contact with the world of objects in order to gain sense gratification. The eyes wish to see beautiful forms and colors, the tongue craves good food, the nose likes to smell pleasant fragrances, and so on. But when we continue to live only for the gratification of our sensual demands, passions multiply and ultimately consume us. To avoid such a condition, discipline (brahmacharya) at the physical level

> The purpose of religion is to eliminate ignorance through spiritual practices until the devotee comes to gain the light of wisdom.

is prescribed. The meaning of the word brahmacharya has been so badly distorted that the real value of this discipline has been lost. Brahmacharya is an attitude of intelligent contact with the world. It does not mean a total denial of sense enjoyments, but only insists on not overdoing anything. Thus to read, watch television, talk, or walk too much, or to eat a morsel more than is necessary would be considered as breaking the vow of brahmacharya. When we live in self-control we discover in ourselves a renewed dynamism, and become pillars of strength in society. If this sacred doctrine is not followed, we abdicate our own freedom and become slaves to the ever-changing circumstances of life. Thus, brahmacharya is a value to be lived at the physical level.

Non-Injury

The second discipline, prescribed for the mental level, is non-injury (ahiṁsa). Ahiṁsa does not simply mean non-killing or non-injury at the physical level. It is to be understood as a mental attitude regarding our relationship with others. Non-injury is the spirit that should dominate the realm of our motives. Sometimes it is necessary that our actions be cruel

> *The three corner stones upon which the temple of Hinduism has been built are self-control, non-injury, and truthfulness.*

although the underlying motive is totally loving and kind. Shakespeare beautifully expressed this idea in Hamlet, "I am cruel only to be kind." For example, a surgeon may outwardly appear to be cruel while performing an operation but his motive is honorable. Such actions, though causing physical pain, would be considered as ahiṁsa. To physically resist a burglar in our homes or standing up to unwise policies of a priest or politician, is not transgressing ahiṁsa. Non-injury is not a passive ineffectual attitude. Restraining the wicked to protect the good is the very creed of every true Hindu.

Thus, non-injury, as advised by the architects of the Hindu culture, is a value of life to be applied at the level of our motives. Our motives should be blessed and pure without any cruelty or hatred. In the execution of a pure motive, we may have to weed out the thorny shrubs to make the garden beautiful again.

Truthfulness

Satyam or truthfulness is the means to govern our inner world of mind and intellect. The outer world is a great university providing us with innumerable opportunities from which to learn. When these experiences have been well churned in our mind and the intellect has come to a firm decision, we must have the honesty and conviction to act upon it. When we do not make full use of our mind and intellect, they lose

> *In the execution of a pure motive, we may have to weed out the thorny shrubs to make the garden beautiful again.*

their efficiency and we suffer as a result. Religion constantly reminds us to exercise our mind and intellect through its insistence upon the principle, "Be truthful to your previously gained wisdom."

Thus, truthfulness enjoins us to live according to our intellectual convictions. We all have ideals, but we often fall prey to our senses and compromise with them. This is dishonest living. Our dignity depends on our ability to live up to our convictions at all times.

The edifice of life stands on these three great principles. By following them we can integrate our personality and gain inner health. It is by this method alone that we can enjoy living in the world and develop the strength and courage to overcome all our problems in life.

When a person has learned to live in perfect self-control, ever vigilant to gather knowledge from life's experiences, practicing non-injury in his motives, and being truthful to his convictions, he becomes the chosen child of nature to be lifted to the top of the evolutionary ladder.

It is true, no doubt, that there are only a few in society who practice these great principles, but those few grow to such a stature that they lead the world with an irresistible spiritual power. It is these people of heroic personality, with integrated head and heart, who will continue to guide humanity to new levels of spiritual evolution.

Questions for Self-Reflection:
1. How do spiritual practices help in eliminating one's ignorance?

2. What are some practical ways to practice Ahimsa?

Coming up Next:

In this next article titled 'Indian Philosophy Helps Us See Clearly, Act Wisely in an Interconnected World', author Matthew MacKenzie explores the Bhagavad Gita and The Mahayana Buddhism book 'Guide to the Awakened Way of Life' by Shantideva. The author explains how both texts describe the notion of the connection between the individual and the broader society and nature. And the wisdom that requires changing one's perception of the world and one's place in it.

25.

Indian Philosophy Helps Us See Clearly, Act Wisely in an Interconnected World

Matthew MacKenzie

To say the world today is interconnected is a cliché.

Never before have so many people been linked by their activities and consequences. But knowing how to think and act as a citizen of this small world is no easy matter.

As the COVID-19 pandemic continues – and Americans worry about their health, loved ones and jobs – it can be difficult to grasp that the crisis began after the coronavirus spread from animal to human on the other side of the planet.

Indian thinkers have been reflecting on interconnectedness for more than two millennia. I study Indian philosophy, and I believe this diverse tradition offers rich and timely insights about how people might better understand global interconnectedness today and act more wisely.

Analysis of the world, from experts

The *'Guide to the Awakened Way of Life'* by Shantideva, an eighth-century Buddhist monk, explores the arduous path from ignorance and suffering to spiritual liberation. For Shantideva and his fellow Mahayana Buddhists – the predominant branch of Buddhism in north and central Asia – this involves cultivating a wise understanding of the interdependence of things and a compassionate concern for all sentient beings.

The Hindu scripture the *Bhagavad Gita*, written between 400 B.C. and 200 A.D., is a classic of world literature. Through the story of the great warrior Arjuna and his friend and spiritual advisor Krishna, the text explores how one's actions in the world can become a path to spiritual freedom.

These texts, which depict the struggle to find freedom in the world, still resonate today.

Seeing Interconnection

In both texts, wisdom requires changing one's perception of the world and one's place in it. One must come to see the world as an interwoven tapestry of cause and effect, and see oneself as part of that tapestry and capable of spiritual freedom within it.

Buddhist thinkers like Shantideva learned to analyze complex things and recognize the network of causes and conditions that give rise to them. As he puts it, "Everything is dependent on something else. Even that thing upon which each is dependent is not independent." The deepest form of wisdom is seeing that all phenomena are empty of any fixed, independent existence. The central message of the 'Guide' is that the awakened life unites the wisdom of interdependence with active compassion for all those who suffer.

> *One must come to see the world as an interwoven tapestry of cause and effect, and see oneself as part of that tapestry and capable of spiritual freedom within it.*

In the *Bhagavad Gita*, the natural world is understood to be a dynamic, evolving tapestry. Our human bodies, minds and actions are inextricable from the larger patterns of cause and effect in nature. Yet the most interesting theme of interconnectedness in the text is not causal but social and moral.

The text opens at the start of a battle between clans for the fate of a kingdom. Describing the scene to his blind king, the seer Sanjaya refers to the battlefield as a field of dharma, the spiritual and moral order that upholds the world. That is, a site of impending conflict, death and chaos is also one of relationship, duty and moral choice.

> Spiritual freedom is waking up from the delusion of being a separate self in conflict with the world. Instead, the wise person realizes that 'all those happy in the world are so because of their desire for the happiness of others.'

This is a central message of the *Bhagavad Gita*. The human world is inextricable from nature. But as a human world it is upheld by our relationships and responsibilities to one another.

The wise person must see his or her own roles – as parent, child, worker, citizen – in light of this field of relationships. Amid war, or the uncertainty and suffering of a pandemic, the central question is: What can I do to uphold right relationships with others?

Engagement As a Path to Freedom

Despite their views on the interconnectedness of the world, classical Indian thinkers were not starry-eyed romantics. They recognized that pain and loss are inescapable. They saw that human selfishness and ignorance are deeply woven in the fabric of life.

Shantideva describes the human situation like this: Hoping to escape suffering, it is to suffering that they run. In the desire for happiness, out of delusion, they cut down their own happiness, like an enemy.

For Indian philosophers, one must see the world clearly in order to act wisely in it. What then, is the wise response to an interconnected world that inevitably includes the good and bad – even pandemics?

For Shantideva, the awakened life is one of altruistic concern for all sentient beings. Spiritual freedom is waking up from the delusion of being a separate self in conflict with the world. Instead, the wise person realizes that "all those happy in the world are so because of their desire for the happiness of others."

> *Action in the world is unavoidable. So rather than obsessing about the 'fruits' of action for oneself, such as praise or blame, one should focus on the moral quality of the action.*

One's own happiness arises from compassion for others. In an interconnected world, Shantideva asks, "In the same way that hands and other limbs are loved because they form part of the body, why are embodied creatures not likewise loved because they form part of the universe?"

In the *Bhagavad Gita*, the key to inner freedom in an uncertain and conflicted world is to change one's focus when acting. Krishna advises Arjuna:

> *"It is in action alone that you have a claim, never at any time to the fruits of such action. Never let the fruits of action be your motive; never let your attachment be to inaction."*

Action in the world is unavoidable. So rather than obsessing about the 'fruits' of action for oneself, such as praise or blame, one should focus on the moral quality of the action.

The *Bhagavad Gita*, highlights three aspects of action one should focus on. Is the action right? Does it serve the welfare of the world? Is it motivated by love? Krishna's message to Arjuna is that, even in battle, wise action consists in giving up selfishness and doing one's duty out of a sense of love and commitment to the common good.

In both texts, the world is understood as an interconnected web of cause and effect, happiness and suffering, life and death. In such a world, acting from ignorance or selfishness leads to suffering for oneself and others. Acting from wisdom and a love for the common good can lead to sense of inner freedom, even in difficult circumstances.

In our interconnected world, everyday actions can have far-reaching consequences. Moreover, as the *Bhagavad Gita*, and the Guide remind us, we are deeply interwoven with one another and the natural world.

Wise freedom is to be found in the midst of this interconnectedness, by the grocery worker keeping people fed, the organizer serving his community, or the doctor treating her patients. Classical texts cannot teach us virology or epidemiology, but they can help us to see our deep interdependence and how to act more wisely and compassionately in light of it.

Questions for Self-Reflection:
1. Is it harder to see connectedness with fellow humans than with the animal and plant kingdom?

2. How is it possible to consolidate the idea of interdependence with independence? Or do they mean the same?

Coming up Next:

In the article 'World Major Religions are Like Branches Growing from One Trunk', author Tom Harpur uncovers remarkable similarities in the teachings of Lord Krishna and Jesus Christ.

26.

World's Major Religions are Like Branches Growing from One Trunk

Tom Harpur

The thing that has struck me most in the study of world religions is that the deeper down you go, the farther back, the closer they come together.

They are like branches stemming from one trunk. There is but one universal mythos (story) behind them all. One way of expressing this is what is called the 'Perennial Philosophy'. The English novelist and essayist, Aldous Huxley (1894-1963), sums that up best in his introduction to a translation of The Song Of God, also known as the *Bhagavad Gita*.

He notes four common doctrines, which denote the basic core or 'Highest Common Factor' I'm talking about. They are:

- The world about us, the world of matter and of individualized consciousness, is the manifestation of a 'Divine Ground' of being within which all else has its existence. As the Bible says, quoting a Pagan source, "In Him we live and move and have our being."
- Humans are capable not just of knowing about this Ground (God) by inference from creation, they can also realize its presence by direct intuition –

a form of knowing superior to ordinary discursive reasoning. This immediate form of knowledge unites the knower and the known.

- We each possess a dual nature; an ordinary ego, and an eternal Self, which is the inner person, the spirit, the spark of divinity within the soul. From a Christian perspective, I would say "the Christ within." It is possible for each to identify with this inner spirit, or Higher Self, and thus with the Divine Ground which is of 'the same or like nature with the spirit'.

- Our life on earth has but one main aim and purpose. It's to identify oneself with one's eternal Self and so come to 'unitive knowledge of the Divine Ground' or God.

Once you are aware of this Perennial Philosophy you can find it in the mystical writings and in all the sacred books of every faith. Many Christians today don't like to encounter this kind of truth because it upsets their view that Christianity was an entirely new and superior religion when it first came on the scene. They believe strongly that things attributed to Jesus – both in word and in deed, from a virgin birth to death on a cross, followed by resurrection – were highly original and definitive for the entire global community for all time.

> *In the study of world religions, the deeper down you go, the farther back, the closer they come together. They are like branches stemming from one trunk. There is but one universal mythos (story) behind them all.*

But, continuous research and wide reading have shown not just to me but to most honest scholars, including Huxley, that this is simply not the case. Reading the New Testament – or watching supposedly accurate portrayals of it on film without any sense of this universal context – totally distorts the truth.

To see what I mean, look at the *Bhagavad Gita*, for example. Krishna, the Hindu Christ, is the major speaker. By the way, the Greek word Christos (it occurs 40 times in the Greek version of the Old Testament, dating back to circa 280 BCE) and the word Krishna both come from a Sanskrit root, 'kr', meaning to anoint. What Krishna says anticipates many of Jesus' pronouncements by centuries – even millennia.

> *Once you are aware of this Perennial Philosophy you can find it in the mystical writings and in all the sacred books of every faith.*

Some examples. Krishna: "Within this body, Life immortal that shall not perish; I am the Truth and the Joy forever." Jesus says in John: "I am the way, the truth and the life."

Krishna: "I am the atman (soul) that dwells in the heart of every creature; I am the beginning, the lifespan and the end of all." Again he says: "In the alphabet, I am A... I am time without end." Jesus says he is the alpha and omega, the beginning and the end.

Krishna tells Arjuna: "Of this be certain, the man that loves Me, he shall not perish." Jesus says: "If you keep my commandments, ye shall abide in my love."

Krishna speaks of himself as "the Lord, who is the light-giver, the highest of the high." Jesus says: "I am the light of world."

Krishna: "Thus think the ignorant that I the unmanifest am become man. They do not know my nature; That is one with Brahman (God, the Father), changeless, superhuman. ... I am not shown to many. How shall this world, bewildered by delusion, recognize me, who am not born and change not?" Jesus says: "I and the Father are one ... no man can know me except it be shown him of my Father." It is also said of him, he is the same "yesterday, today, and forever."

Krishna: "I am the Word that is God... the Light of the fire, Life of all lives..."

John's Gospel says that Jesus is the Logos or Word, the true light by which all was created.

Krishna: "The world fails to recognize me as I really am. I stand apart from them all, supreme and deathless." Jesus says: "The world cannot hate you; but me it hateth..."

We badly need this kind of context to media coverage of religion today.

Questions for Self-Reflection:

1. All religions fundamentally share a perennial philosophy based on mystical writing and revelations of their own saints and prophets. Why is it then most of the conflict in the world appears to stem from religion – specifically religious fundamentalism?

2. There are remarkable similarities between the sayings of Lord Krishna and Jesus Christ, especially when one carefully compares the underlying perennial philosophy in the Bhagavad Gita and the Holy Bible respectively. What are the possible exchanges of ideas between far away lands in the ancient past?

About the Authors

Caroline Castrillon

Caroline Castrillon is a career and life coach who helps people go from soul-sucking job to career fulfillment and is the founder of Corporate Escape Artist. Prior to Corporate Escape Artist, she has held executive leadership roles in small tech firms as well as Fortune 500 companies including Dell and Sony.

Chitra Banerjee Divakaruni

Chitra Banerjee Divakaruni is an award-winning and bestselling author, activist, and professor. Her work has been published in over fifty magazines, including *The Atlantic* and *The New Yorker,* and included in *The Best American Short Stories and The O. Henry Prize Stories.* Her books have been translated into twenty-nine languages, including Dutch, Hebrew, Bengali, Russian, and Japanese. Several have been used for campus vide reads and made into films and plays. She teaches at the University of Houston.

Vivek Gupta

Vivek Gupta is the Resident Teacher of Chinmaya Mission Niagara and Deputy Director of Chinmaya Yuva Kendra West, a wing of the organization dedicated to empowering youth and young adults. His unifying and universal vision has led him to communities and organizations all around the world.

Tom Harpur

Tom Harpur, Rhodes scholar and Anglican priest, was a prominent writer on religious and ethical issues. He authored seven best-selling books including *For Christ's Sake*, and *Would You Believe?* He passed away in 2017 at the age of 87 years.

Kimberly Kirberger

Kimberly Kirberger is the president and founder of I.A.M. for Teens, Inc. (Inspiration and Motivation for Teens, Inc.) a corporation formed exclusively to work for teens. It is her goal to see teens represented in a more positive light and it is her strong belief that teens deserve better and more positive treatment.

Ichiro Kishimi

Ichiro Kishimi was born in Kyoto, where he currently resides. He writes and lectures on Adlerian psychology and provides counseling for youth in psychiatric clinics as a certified counselor and consultant for the Japanese Society of Adlerian Psychology.

Fumitake Koga

Fumitake Koga is an award-winning professional writer and author. He has released numerous bestselling works of business-related and general non-fiction. He encountered Adlerian psychology in his late twenties and was deeply affected by its conventional wisdom defying ideas.

Matthew MacKenzie

Matthew MacKenzie is Professor of Philosophy and Department Chair at Colorado State University. He specializes in Buddhist philosophy, classical Indian philosophy, and the philosophy of mind. His articles have appeared in *Philosophy East and West, Phenomenology and the Cognitive Sciences, Asian Philosophy*, and *Journal of Consciousness Studies*, among other journals.

Nasim Mansuri

Nasim Mansuri is passionate about the written word and its role in the betterment of society. Originally from Paraguay, she has served in Baha'i community building efforts in many countries since childhood. She has a Bachelor of Science in Chemical Engineering and Professional Writing from Worcester Polytechnic Institute, and currently lives in Massachusetts, where she is engaged in establishing a strong junior youth and children's spiritual empowerment program with the local community.

Gabriela Díaz Musmanni

Gabriela Díaz Musmanni is a highly skilled NGO communications professional (English/Spanish) with global experience and a passion for environmental causes, humanitarian issues and yoga. She has worked for NGOs and UN agencies in different capacities in the field of communications and environmental causes. She also has a lengthy journalism background, as the environment and human rights reporter for an English newspaper in Costa Rica.

Dean Ornish

Dean Ornish is an American physician and researcher. He is the president and founder of the nonprofit Preventive Medicine Research Institute in Sausalito, California, and a Clinical Professor of Medicine at the University of California, San Francisco. The author of *Dr. Dean Ornish's Program for Reversing Heart Disease, Eat More, Weigh Less* and *The Spectrum*, he is an advocate for using diet and lifestyle changes to treat and prevent heart disease.

Peace Pilgrim

From 1953 to 1981 a silver-haired woman calling herself only 'Peace Pilgrim' walked more than 25,000 miles on a personal pilgrimage for peace. She vowed to "remain a wanderer until mankind has learned the way of peace, walking until given shelter and fasting until given food." In the course of her 28-year pilgrimage she touched the hearts, minds, and lives of thousands of individuals all across North America. She passed away in 1981 at the age of 73 years.

Cherie´ Carter-Scott

New York Times #1 Best Selling author Cherie´ Carter-Scott, Ph.D. has been coaching change successfully since 1974. Dr. Carter-Scott is an international author, entrepreneur, consultant, lecturer, teacher/trainer, talk-show host, and seminarleader.Hercompany,MotivationManagementService Institute,Inc.(MMS),hasreachedmillionsofpeopleworldwide.

Mark Sorbara

Mark Sorbara has a BA. in History from Queen's University (Canada) and a master's degree in politics of Sub-Saharan Africa from the School of Oriental and African Studies (UK). He was also principal Africa researcher in office of the deputy chair of Canada's Senate standing committee on foreign affairs while it completed a study on Africa's security and development.

Swami Ajaya

Swami Ajaya, was initiated in 1973 as a Swami in the Himalayan tradition by Swami Rama. This initiation took place in Rishikesh, on the banks of the Ganges, on Shivaratri, a sacred holy day. As Swami Ajaya, he spent years in India studying and teaching yoga and meditation. He has authored and edited several landmark texts that integrate Eastern and Western approaches to healing the whole person.

Swami Chinmayananda

Swami Chinmayananda known to his followers as Gurudev, was born in 1916 in Kerala, India, and is pre-eminent among the wave of Vedantic teachers who emerged in the 1940s following the expansion of Vedanta to the West by Swami Vivekananda. He is a direct disciple of world-renowned Vedantic luminaries Swami Sivananda and Swami Tapovan of Uttarkashi. Swami Chinmayananda is credited with the renaissance of spirituality and cultural values in India because of his modern and dynamic approach to the spread of the ageless wisdom of Advaita Vedanta, as expounded by Adi Shankaracharya. Swami Chinmayananda attained mahasamadhi on August 3, 1993 at the age of 77 years.

Swami Jyotirmayananda

Swami Jyotirmayananda was born on February 3, 1931 in Bihar, India. He embraced the ancient order of sanyasa on February 3, 1953 at the age of 22. He served his guru, Swami Sivananda tirelessly. In March 1969 he established an ashram in Miami, Florida, the Yoga Research Foundation that has become the center for international activities. Branches of this organization now exist throughout the world.

Swami Purushottamananda

Swami Purushottamananda served at the Ramakrishna Mission Bangalore Centre for about 30 years. In 2000 he took over as president of the newly affiliated Ramakrishna Mission Ashram at Belgaum. Swamiji was instrumental in the setting up of several voluntary organizations, Satsanga, as well as private Ramakrishna Ashramas throughout Karnataka. He took a very active role in spreading the message of Shri Ramakrishna, Shri Sarada Devi, and Swami Vivekananda, through his discourses, bhajans, and Satsanga programs. Swami Purushottamananda attained mahasamadhi in 2005 at the age of 74 years.

Swami Rama

Swami Rama was the founder of The Himalayan Institute. He was a leader in the field of yoga, meditation, spirituality, and holistic health. The mission of the Himalayan Institute is to discover and embrace the sacred link – the spirit of human heritage that unites East and West, spirituality and science, and ancient wisdom and modern technology. He passed away in 1996 at the age of 71 years.

Swami Tejomayananda

Swami Tejomayananda, Head of Chinmaya Mission Worldwide from 1993 to 2017, is one of the Mission's preeminent senior teachers in India, teaching in Hindi and English. Fondly addressed as Guruji and described by his own guru as an exquisite teacher, Swamiji, in his teaching, combines the erudite and penetrating vision of an established exponent of Advaita Vedanta with the soft heart of a bhakti yogi. Swami Tejomayananda continues the missionary work of his guru, offering Vedānta jnana yajnas throughout India, publishing commentaries on the Upanishads and other key texts. Guruji also sponsors cultural revival through the patronage of an exemplary and prestigious program of music and dance at Chinmaya Vibhuti, the Mission's cultural center in Maharashtra state.

Harold Taylor

Harold Taylor is the owner of Taylor In Time. He developed time management training aids, products, cassettes and video programs including the popular Taylor Time Planner. He has been a popular guest on radio and television throughout Canada and the United States.

Eckhart Tolle

Eckhart Tolle is widely recognized as one of the most inspiring and visionary spiritual teachers in the world today. With his international bestsellers, The Power of Now and A New Earth – translated into 52 languages – he has introduced millions to the joy and freedom of living life in the present moment. The New York Times has described him as "the most popular spiritual author in the United States", and in 2011, Watkins

Review named him "the most spiritually influential person in the world".

Vinita Hampton Wright

Vinita Hampton Wright has edited books for Loyola Press, a Jesuit ministry, for 21 years, serving as managing editor in recent years. She has published her own fiction and nonfiction, including the most recent *Small Simple Ways: An Ignatian Daybook for Healthy Spiritual Living.*

Dada Jashan P. Vaswani

Dada Jashan P. Vaswani was the spiritual head of Sadhu Vaswani Mission in Pune, India. He was born on August 2, 1918, at Hyderabad-Sind, in a pious Sindhi family. He is credited to have started the first all girl's college, St. Mira's College, which now has an enrollment of 5000 students. He authored about 30 books in English and several more in Sindhi. He passed away in 2018 at the age of 91 years.

Transliteration and Pronunciation Guide

In the book, Devanāgarī characters are transliterated according to the scheme adopted by the International Congress of Orientalists at Athens in 1912. In it, one fixed pronunciation value is given to each letter; f, q, w, x, and z are not called to use. An audio recording of this guide is available at www.chinmayamission.com/scriptures.php. According to this scheme:

	sounds like		sounds like
'	a silent 'a'	l	l in love
a	o in son	ḷ	**
ā	a in father	m	m in mind
ai	i in delight	ṁ	m in improvise
au	o in now	n	n in nose
b	b in boil	ṅ	an in ankle*
bh	bh in abhor	ṇ	n in under*
c	ch in chuckle	ñ	ny in banyan
ch	ch in witch*	o	o in core
d	th in this	p	p in pen
ḍ	d in dog	ph	ph in phantom*
dh	dh in Gandhi	r	r in right
ḍh	dh in adhesive	ṛ	rh in rhythm*
e	a in evade	ṝ	**
g	g in gate	s	in simple
gh	gh in ghost	ṣ	in sugar
h	h in happy	ś	sh in shut
ḥ	**	t	t in tabla
i	i in different	ṭ	t in tank
ī	ee in feet	th	th in thumb
j	j in just	ṭh	**
jh	jh in Jhansi	tr	th in three*
jñ	gn in gnosis	u	u in full
k	c in calm	ū	oo in boot
kh	kh in khan	v	v in very
kṣ	tio in action	y	y in yes

---

* These letters do not have an exact English equivalent. An approximation is given here.

** These sounds cannot be approximated in English words.

About Mananam

The Sanskrit word mananam means 'reflection'. The Mananam Series of books is dedicated to promoting the ageless wisdom of Vedānta, with an emphasis on the unity of all religions. Spiritual teachers from different traditions give us fresh, insightful answers to age-old questions so that we may apply them in practical ways to the dilemmas we all face in life. Mananam is published twice yearly by Chinmaya Mission West, which was founded by Swami Chinmayananda in 1975.

Swami Chinmayananda pursued the spiritual path in the Himalayas under the guidance of Swami Sivananda and Swami Tapovan. He is credited with the awakening of India and the rest of the world to the ageless wisdom of Vedānta. He taught the logic of spirituality and emphasized that selfless work, study, and meditation are the cornerstones of spiritual practice. His legacy remains in the form of books, audio and video recordings, schools, social service projects, and Vedānta teachers, who now serve their local communities all around the world.

THE mananam SERIES

The list of prior publications contd...

Emotions

Service: An Act of Worship

Vision of the Bhagavad Gita

The Journey Called Life

The Light of Wisdom

Reincarnation: The Karmic Cycle

Maya: The Divine Power

Embracing Love

At Home in the Universe

Beyond Ego

Happiness Through Integration

Living in Simplicity

Timeless Values

The Path of Love

Mind: Our Greatest Gift

The Sages Speak About Immortality

The Sages Speak About Life & Death

Divine Songs: The Gitas of India

Religion and Spirituality

Time and Beyond

About Sadhana

Divine Grace

Spirituality in Family Life

The Divine Mother

Beyond Stress

The Power of Faith

Joy: Our True Nature

Contemplation in a World of Action

Love and Forgiveness

Saints and Mystics

Om: The Symbol of Truth

The Illusory Ego

The Source of Inspiration

The Essential Teacher

The Razor's Edge

Harmony and Beauty

The Question of Freedom

The Pursuit of Happiness

On the Path

Beyond Sorrow

Self-Discovery

The Mystery of Creation

Vedanta in Action

Solitude

THE mananam SERIES

(Mananam – Sanskrit for 'Reflection upon the Truth')
Prior publications listed in sequence (most recent listed first)

THE mananam SERIES

WRITINGS FROM THE SPIRITUAL TRADISTIONS OF THE WORLD

Don't miss the next issue!

To Subscribe for Mananam Books:
https://www.chinmayapublications.com/mananam

To Purchase Mananam Books:
https://www.chinmayapublications.com/mananam-series

NOTES

NOTES